Wildfire

A CODE RED ADVENTURE

CHRIS RYAN

RED FOX

WILDFIRE
A RED FOX BOOK 978 1 862 30166 5 (from January 2007)
1 862 30166 2

First published in 2006

First published in Great Britain in 2007 by Red Fox,
an imprint of Random House Children's Books

1 3 5 7 9 10 8 6 4 2

Set in Sabon

Red Fox Books are published by Random House Children's Books,
61–63 Uxbridge Road, London W5 5SA,
a division of The Random House Group Ltd,
in Australia by Random House Australia (Pty) Ltd,
20 Alfred Street, Milsons Point, Sydney, NSW 2061, Australia,
in New Zealand by Random House New Zealand Ltd,
18 Poland Road, Glenfield, Auckland 10, New Zealand,
in South Africa by Random House (Pty) Ltd,
Isle of Houghton, Corner Boundary Road & Carse O'Gowrie,
Houghton 2198, South Africa,
and in India by Random House India Pvt Ltd,
301 World Trade Tower, Hotel Intercontinental Grand Complex,
Barakhamba Lane, New Delhi 110001, India

THE RANDOM HOUSE GROUP Limited Reg. No. 954009

www.kidsatrandomhouse.co.uk

A CIP catalogue record for this book is available from the British Library.

Printed and bound in Great Britain by
Cox & Wyman Ltd, Reading, Berkshire

Kelly grabbed him and shrieked, 'Fire!'

A mass of tumbling, burning branches blasted towards them.

They turned and hared back the way they'd come. It was uphill, and strenuous going in the strong mid-afternoon heat. Ben could feel the smoke in his throat. It was hard to get his breath but adrenaline gave him a burst of speed.

Kelly looked back. From the vantage point of the brow of the hill, she saw a wall of flame stretching right across the vineyard. The wind was fanning it towards them.

'The whole place is on fire!' she yelled. 'We can't outrun it!'

Also by Chris Ryan:

The Code Red Adventures
FLASH FLOOD

The Alpha Force Series
SURVIVAL
RAT-CATCHER
DESERT PURSUIT
HOSTAGE
RED CENTRE
HUNTED
BLOOD MONEY
FAULT LINE
BLACK GOLD
UNTOUCHABLE

A CODE RED ADVENTURE

Location: Adelaide, Australia

Chapter One

Matt Forrest turned off the engine of the green John Deere tractor and climbed down from the cab. It was barely nine in the morning but already the temperature had to be nearly forty degrees. Behind Matt, twenty-one hectares of vineyard spread up the valley in neat green rows, standing out against the red South Australian earth. To his left the white grapes showed faintly gold in the bleaching sunshine. To his right, black grapes made purple speckles among the green vines.

This summer had been one of the hottest and driest on record. Now it was finally February, the beginning of autumn, and the grapes at Forrest Vale vineyard were ready to harvest.

The harvest was always a special occasion for Matt and Jenny. Friends, neighbours, family and extended family came from miles around to help. For the next two weeks the couple's wooden ranch-style house, which nestled at the bottom of the valley, would be full of guests.

Matt took off his bush hat and wiped the sweat out of his eyes, then stepped up onto the wooden decking that ran along the back of the house. Jenny was down at the local store getting supplies for the buffet lunch that would welcome the workers. It was Matt's job to set up the tables and chairs.

He took two folding chairs from the stack leaning against the kitchen door and set them out on the stretch of grass in front of the decking. He went back, got two more, turned round—

And stopped. He couldn't believe his eyes. Moments ago the hillside had been bathed in fierce sunshine as usual. But now the sky was turning black. The vines, completely still a moment ago, stirred as though an invisible hand was ruffling through them.

It was going to rain. Heavily.

Matt hurried back under cover. He was just in time. The rain came thundering down, making a deafening sound on the wooden roof.

Matt was stunned. It had been a lifelessly still morning. Now it was like sitting under a waterfall. He and Jenny had spent most of the season watching the weather forecast religiously. First, worried that the drought would kill the vines, they had spent a fortune watering them. Now that the vines were mature, rain could make the grapes rot, and so they had been praying for the dry spell to continue. One thing Matt was sure of: no storm had been forecast for today.

Above the noise of the rain he heard another sound. The phone. He ran into the kitchen and snatched up the receiver.

It was Jenny. 'Hi, honey. I got everything except the ice. Do you think we can manage without it?'

Matt could barely hear her, the sound of the rain was so loud.

'Are you driving in this?' He had to shout.

'Driving in what?' replied Jenny. 'Why are you shouting?'

Through the window Matt couldn't even see the vines, just a thick rust-red fog. Above, the sky was an angry stripe of black. The rain was coming down with such a force that it was stirring up the dust in the valley like feet stirring up muck at the bottom of a pond. Surely Jenny wouldn't even be able to see through the windscreen.

'Honey, don't try to drive in this. Pull over until it stops.'

'Until what's stopped?'

'The rain!' shouted Matt.

'What rain?' said Jenny. 'It's fine here. Bright sunshine. The weather forecast said there'd be no change.'

'It's coming down in buckets here,' said Matt. He looked out of the window. Hailstones were pounding onto the decking, hard as golf balls. 'Can't you hear that?'

'I just thought it was a bad line,' said Jenny. 'I'll be back in five minutes. Bye.'

Matt was baffled.

Outside, the two chairs had been knocked over. Matt looked up at the sky and dashed out to rescue them. The wind flung sand in his face. His neck and arms stung as though pins were being thrown at him.

He dived back out of the rain.

And then, as suddenly as it had started, the storm stopped. The strong sun came out and the sky brightened. In under a minute it was deep blue again. The clouds of red dust slowly settled.

Matt leaned the chairs up against one of the posts that supported the roof.

That was when he noticed another strange thing. The chairs weren't wet at all. They were, however, covered in powdery red dust.

So were his Brasher work boots.

He took off his hat. The brim was full of dust and pebbles. But no hailstones.

There was no water anywhere, not even a trail of wet footprints where he had come in. The wooden decking was bone-dry. So was he.

How was that possible?

Matt stepped out onto the grass. It was covered in dust, and thousands of stones. Some were the size of Matt's hand. They must have come from somewhere out in the desert.

That hadn't been a rainstorm after all.

It had been a *dust* storm. A freak tornado – which had gone as suddenly as it had appeared . . .

Some summer days are just too hot.

February half term in Adelaide, Australia, was startlingly different from England. The sun was shining brightly and the temperature was over forty degrees.

Most sensible people were indoors with the air conditioning on full. But right now, English teenager Ben Tracey was out under the glaring sun. He was clad from neck to ankles in a flying suit and his ears were muffled with big headphones like a pair of black foam doughnuts.

It was an outfit that would normally have been unbearably hot in those conditions, but Ben was feeling cold. Cold with fear.

He was about to go flying in a Microlight Thruster.

It wasn't the flying that bothered him. On the contrary, he'd just spent most of the last twenty hours in a jumbo jet. He had been in the central section, and the wings and the cockpit had seemed so far away that he could have been sitting in a row of seats in the departure lounge. It didn't feel much like flying at all.

But this microlight was a little too much at the other extreme.

For a start, it was tiny. The whole thing looked home-made – and not very strongly. The cockpit was a fibreglass pod attached to a hang-glider wing by a series of struts like a child's climbing frame. Cables passed between the two seats, connecting pedals at the front to flaps at the back. They looked like they could easily be snipped in two with a pair of wirecutters. The undercarriage consisted of three wheels like a tricycle. Behind the seats, the pod was open to the elements. Ben had seen model aeroplanes that looked more substantial.

Now they were trundling out along the tarmac airstrip, taxiing to the runway. Ben could feel every bump in the concrete. The two-stroke engine, mounted in the middle of the wing above his head, sounded like it had been pinched from a lawnmower. The propeller paddled in a lazy circle like a ceiling fan.

He'd heard of light aircraft but this was ridiculous. If this thing got into the air he'd be amazed.

The bleached concrete of the airstrip was marked with painted chevrons and arrows. Beyond the perimeter wire lay dusty, scrubby brush, and in the distance the parched hills of the vineyards of South Australia. The way the engine was burping and stuttering gave Ben an alarming vision of the microlight bobbing up and down through the air for a mile or two and then crashing into the vineyards. If that happened, he hoped the rows of vines would break their fall.

What was worse than the flimsy aircraft and the lawnmower engine was that Ben knew the pilot didn't really want him there. She was a blonde, eighteen-year-old Texan girl called Kelly, and she clearly wasn't thrilled at having a thirteen-year-old as a passenger.

'Most people find microlights pretty scary,' Kelly said through his headset as she completed her pre-flight checks. 'If you want, you can get out and watch first.'

'No thanks,' said Ben. 'I want to go up.'

But he kept noticing more things that added to his apprehension. There was the brake handle, for instance. It looked like a bicycle brake on a stick

8

poking out of the floor. For some reason a Velcro strap was hanging off it. And then there was the door. It had a rotating catch that was so fiddly he hadn't been able to close it when he first got in. Kelly had watched him fumble with it, then impatiently batted his hands out of the way and fastened it herself. Now he kept wondering if it was about to come undone.

Kelly consulted the map spread out on her knee, then spoke to the control tower through the mouthpiece. 'This is microlight Tango Eight Five Sierra Golf. Requesting permission to take off.'

Ben heard their reply. '*Go ahead, Tango Eight Five Sierra Golf. Take off runway zero-nine under your own discretion.*'

'Ben,' said Kelly, 'we're going up. Last chance if you wanna get out. Oh, and don't touch those pedals or that handle beside you or we'll crash.'

Ben had a set of pedals in his foot well and a lever between him and the door. He made sure his hands and feet were well away from them. But he did it casually, as though he wasn't worried. It was clear that Kelly would like nothing better than for him to bottle out.

Sweat trickled from the heavy foam pads around his ears and down into his collar. Kelly pushed the centre stick forward and opened the throttle. The lawn-mower engine gave a roar. The white propeller became a blur. Suddenly the machine was moving forward with purpose.

They gathered speed, then Kelly pulled the stick back and the nose came up. Ben realized the ride had suddenly got smoother. He could no longer feel the wheels on the runway.

They were in the air.

They climbed steeply. Over the parched scrubland and the corduroy vineyards. Over a road, which shrank to a narrow ribbon. A lone van was trundling down it, the size of a grain of rice. Ben's entire body was rigid, waiting for disaster.

Kelly levelled out the craft to cruising altitude. A breeze blew in through the back of the open cockpit behind Ben, making him glad he was wearing the fly-ing suit. It also made him feel like he was dangling from a giant kite. But they were flying, really flying, in a way you could never experience inside an airliner.

A huge grin spread across Ben's face. This was

awesome. He looked across at Kelly and gave her a double thumbs-up.

He didn't see what she did next. Suddenly Ben's stomach left the flying suit. They were slipping sideways and downwards – fast. His shoulder and hip slid across the seat and banged into the door. The ribbon road was zooming towards them. The engine wailed in his ears like in films he'd seen of Second World War Spitfires plummeting to the ground.

Just as abruptly, they were flying level again, gliding through beautiful deep blue sky, the engine purring gently above their heads.

Ben let go of the seat and breathed a long, silent sigh of relief. Well, at least his door had held.

Kelly's eyes were shining. Her face had lost the unfriendly scowl; instead she was glowing with pride. 'That,' she said, 'is crossing the controls. What do you think of my baby flying machine?'

Ben nodded emphatically before he got his brain in gear to reply. The machine might look like a shaky contraption on the ground, but in the air it was magic. 'Amazing,' he said. 'Can I have a go?'

'Maybe,' said Kelly.

Chapter Two

A few hours earlier . . .

Ben had thought Australia would be a nice change from England in February. The small town of Macclesfield in Cheshire, where he lived with his dad, was at its least appealing in winter. The days were short; in fact, they never properly got light. It drizzled all the time. The sky was the colour of dishwater. It was so cold you had to wrap up like an arctic explorer when you went out.

Then his mum had phoned. She and Ben's dad had separated years before and she now travelled the world as a roving ambassador for the environmental organization Fragile Planet. Right now she was in Adelaide, South Australia to speak at a conference on weather science. Would Ben like to come out to stay with her for half term? Ben jumped at the chance. It was a long way to go for just seven days, but Ben couldn't wait to wear flip-flops on the beach, try his hand at surfing, and relax beside the barbecue in the long, warm evenings.

But, he thought as he first arrived in the country, so far it wasn't turning out to be the wonderful experience he had hoped for. For a start, the flight was delayed and his mum couldn't meet him at the airport because she had to give an important speech at the environmental conference. Instead, when he stepped off the plane, he saw a woman in the airline uniform holding up a placard with his name on. She guided him through arrivals and took him outside to get a taxi. He had just a few seconds to bask in the southern hemisphere warmth and look up at the blue sky before she shepherded him into a car with air conditioning so extreme it could have started an ice age.

His escort got into the back seat beside Ben. On the

journey into town she gave him a frightening list of dos and don'ts for his stay in Adelaide.

'Don't go out without sunscreen, ever. Reapply it every two hours. Set your watch or your Blackberry or your phone to remind you so you don't forget. Cover up your arms and legs. Drink plenty of water. Don't go on a journey unless you have high-factor sunscreen and water with you. Ditto if you play sports. Try not to be outside anyway between eleven in the morning and three in the afternoon. Familiarize yourself with the symptoms of heat exhaustion and dehydration; it's all in this leaflet' – she handed him a folded piece of paper – 'so make sure you read it. Don't touch any spiders or caterpillars; there's a section about them in the leaflet too. Don't use hose pipes – we're having the worst drought since records began. Don't light any fires, for any reason, anywhere.'

Ben's brain was reeling with all these instructions, but this one pulled him up short. Fires? he thought. What are the teens around here like?

At the hotel he was briskly hustled up the steps and into the air-conditioned reception. Finally he was left in his room with instructions to unpack and wait for a call.

The room looked out over pale beaches and the sparkling blue marina. The sands were empty; no sun-bathers, but it was ten on a Monday morning, so most people would be at work. There were lifeguards out in the bay and people working on the boats in the marina. During an English summer, people working outdoors in the sunshine wore as little as possible, but here they wore long sleeves, long trousers and hats with wide brims. Cars went by in the street below. More than half of them had soft tops or sun roofs, but they were all closed. So were the windows.

People here didn't welcome the sun. They hid from it.

This was South Australia. Not far away was the infamous hole in the ozone layer. In this part of the world, the sun wasn't a benevolent relief from the cold; it was a cosmic blowtorch.

Ben's mother would have scolded him for forgetting that. Anyone who took the environment for granted, or didn't seem to be taking enough care of it, felt the rough edge of her tongue. Dr Bel Kelland didn't balk at haranguing popes and presidents, and the way she spoke to world leaders on television gave the impression she thought of them as spoiled children with too many toys. Bel was a woman on a mission, all right. She wanted to make her mark on the world. Although, more accurately, you might say she wanted to stop other people making their mark on it. Sometimes Ben was proud of her, but just as often the things she did embarrassed him.

Ben's father, Russell Tracey, wasn't like Bel at all. He was brilliant but shy, happy with his quiet, uneventful life in a small town in Cheshire. Russell and Bel were both scientists, but in every other way they were poles apart, as opposite as the climates of England and Australia in February.

Ben looked at his watch. Bel was supposed to meet him at the hotel room after he'd unpacked. She was late.

He read the leaflet he'd been given. It was a list of the venomous spiders and caterpillars and how to recognize them:

The redback will pretend to be dead rather than bite you, but the funnel-web, which is the size of your palm, will kill you within an hour. The funnel-web will grip its victim and bite several times ...

Despite the constant warnings about sunstroke and dangerous wildlife, Ben was anxious to get out and see the sights. He hadn't spent twenty hours on a plane just to be stuck in a refrigerated hotel room behind tinted glass windows. He was tired but there was no way he could go to sleep when there was so much out there to explore. He started to pace around the room impatiently, wondering how long it would be before he got a message from Bel.

At the same time, Kelly Kurtis was also wondering where *her* parent had got to.

She was walking up the stairs in the Adelaide conference centre, looking for her father and attracting rather a lot of attention. All the people around her were dressed smartly, and wore name tags. Kelly, on the other hand, was wearing an orange baseball cap and pale blue flying overalls, the legs rolled up to her knees like long shorts and the top half unzipped with the arms tied around her waist and a thin vest visible. Her bare arms were slathered in sun-tan oil, which gave off a scent of coconut. Around her neck she had a gold and black scarf. The conference delegates were looking at her as though wondering which planet she'd blown in from – or if she was there to cause trouble.

She pitied them, having to spend all day cooped up in a gloomy conference centre. It was such a lovely day to go flying.

Following the smell of coffee, she took the stairs to the first floor. A cafeteria area with tables and chairs overlooked the main entrance hall below. Then she spotted her dad, sitting at a table at the far end. He was bent over some papers, talking to a woman in a pale-green, slightly crumpled safari suit. A specialist in weather science with the US army, he was wearing dress uniform, charcoal-blue with gold buttons, and a shirt and tie. His dark hair was cut brutally short, military style. Kelly made her way over to them.

Major Brad Kurtis looked up, surprised to see his daughter. 'Kelly! What are you doing here?'

'Hi, Dad. Did you take the keys to the Jeep this morning?'

The major patted his breast pockets absent-mindedly. The left one made a jangling noise. 'Oh yes.' He fished the keys out and handed them over. 'Sorry.'

Kelly took the keys, but now something else had caught her attention. There was something familiar about the woman sitting next to her father, her delicate fingers counting through a stack of papers like the legs of a spider. She was very petite, with straight red hair and an angular chin.

The woman looked up at that moment. Her eyes were icy blue. They registered that Kelly was staring. Kelly gave a slightly uncertain smile. Small though she was, there was something a bit fierce about the woman.

The major snapped his fingers. 'Where are my manners?' He turned to the woman. 'Bel, this is my daughter Kelly. Kelly, this is Bel. Bel Kelland.'

The red-haired woman put out her hand and shook Kelly's. 'Pleased to meet you.' She had an English accent. That and the name – printed in full on the badge she was wearing – suddenly made a connection in Kelly's brain.

BEL KELLAND, FRAGILE PLANET. Kelly suddenly knew where she had seen her before.

'Dr Bel Kelland? You presented the Discovery Channel programme on the flooding of London.' Kelly slipped the Jeep keys into the button-down pocket on her leg, pulled out a chair and sat down. 'I really enjoyed that programme; it was powerful stuff. It's a pleasure to meet you.'

Bel smiled. 'Glad you appreciated it. I was just in the right place at the right time. Or the wrong place at the right time, depending on how you look at it.'

Kelly folded her arms in front of her on the table and leaned forward. 'I had some friends who were in New Orleans when it flooded. Can you get Discovery to do a programme about that? I think you'd be great at it.'

'They've already made one,' said Bel, 'but they got an American environmentalist to front it. Which is a pity, as there were loads of things I wanted to say about the federal government's criminal culpability.' She shrugged. 'Still, I'm always available for weddings, bar mitzvahs and funerals.'

Kelly was baffled for a moment. Was that last remark a joke? She didn't always get the English sense of humour. She laughed uneasily.

The major changed the subject. 'Kelly's travelling before she goes to Stanford in the fall to study law. She got her pilot's licence last year.'

Bel's face became animated. 'Flying?! I got my licence years ago. I love it. I just don't get enough time to do it now.'

Kelly was delighted to find she had something in common with Bel. 'You should come up with me,' she said. 'Dad's hired a microlight while I'm here, and it's got dual controls. Give me a call and I'll take you for a spin.'

'That's very kind of you. I would really, really love to.' Bel spread her hand out over the papers on the table. 'But I'm snowed under here: they want me to chair all the debates and I've got to do a live TV broadcast in a few minutes. My son arrived from England this morning and I don't know how I'm ever going to find time to see him.'

The fierce and feisty Dr Kelland had a son. Kelly had a vision of Bel's delicate features translated into young male form. She imagined a willowy English poet with intense blue eyes, passionate beliefs and a clever, slightly baffling sense of humour. Fresh off the plane and needing a companion. It sounded very appealing.

'I'll take him up in the microlight,' she offered.

Bel was taken aback. 'Would you?'

'Yeah,' said Kelly. 'He can have a go at the controls. I've taken friends up with me loads of times and let them have a go once we're in the air. No problem.'

'That's really kind of you, Kelly. Thank you very much. He'd love it.'

'Is he in TV too?' asked Kelly.

'Oh no,' said Bel, 'he's a bit young for that. He's still at school.'

'In school?' said Kelly. 'Where? Oxford?'

'Not university,' said Bel. 'What you call high school.'

The penny dropped. Kelly now remembered that in England, school meant something different from what it meant in the States.

The major started laughing. 'How old did you say he was, Bel? Fourteen?' They had obviously swapped stories about their children before Kelly arrived.

Bel shook her head. 'Thirteen.'

Kelly felt like a cruel joke had been played on her. 'Thirteen?' she repeated. Her mind's eye wiped out the mental image of a lean young man and replaced it with a tousle-haired freckly swot in an ill-fitting blazer.

'I'm sure he'd love to go up with you, Kels,' said the major. 'You've got the microlight for a month. A couple of days won't hurt.'

Kelly tried to hide the disgust on her face. Taking a thirteen-year-old flying was babysitting. But she couldn't complain too much as her dad was paying for it – and now she'd already made the offer. 'All right,' she said.

Bel's phone rang. 'Excuse me,' she said, 'I have to take this . . . Dr Kelland here . . . OK, see you down-stairs in five minutes.' She closed the phone and slipped it into her breast pocket. 'The ABC Television crew have arrived. I must go.' She got to her feet and gathered up her papers. 'Kelly, it's lovely to meet you, and thanks for agreeing to take Ben up. He'll really enjoy it. He's just like me; he should pick it up with no problem.' She shook Kelly briskly by the hand again. 'He's very grown up.' She made to move away from the table.

'Where will I find him?' asked Kelly.

'Oh yes,' said Bel absent-mindedly. 'He's at the East Beach Hotel. Just ask for him at reception. His name's Ben Tracey.' She thought for a moment, then added: 'He was in London with me when it flooded. He had a hell of an adventure. You can ask him all about it. I've got to dash now. Brad, I'll see you at the first debate.'

Major Kurtis raised a hand to wave her goodbye.

Kelly watched Bel make her way through the crowd towards the stairs. She couldn't imagine what she'd talk to a thirteen-year-old about, even if he had been in a disaster zone. Whichever way she looked at it, she'd been conned into babysitting. But at least the woman had had the decency to look faintly embarrassed about it.

She went back to their hotel, collected the Jeep, and in ten minutes was marching into the foyer of Ben's hotel on the waterfront.

There was a tall guy standing at the reception desk with his back to her. 'I'm waiting for Dr Bel Kelland,' he said to the receptionist. 'Has she left a message?' He had a cool English accent.

Kelly went and stood next to him. 'Do you know Dr Kelland? Because I've got to babysit her kid.'

The guy turned round slowly and looked at her. 'Babysit?' he repeated.

Kelly suddenly realized he was a lot younger than she'd thought. She wished the ground would open up and swallow her. 'Are you Ben?'

Ben's blue eyes narrowed. 'Yes. Who on earth are you?'

Chapter Three

The stage of the conference centre had been set up with two big red chairs. It was the Jonny Cale interview slot and the chairs were his trademark. Each morning he picked somebody who was in the news and interviewed them.

Bel hadn't seen Jonny Cale's work before, but one look at the set-up told her his style might not be in-depth journalism. She sat in the chair, a microphone clipped to her green lapel, and waited for the first question.

Jonny watched the director count down, then turned to the camera and went into his introduction.

'I saw an interesting bit of graffiti on my way in today. I was in the dunny, and I'll spare you any more details, but next to the toilet roll someone had written "Weather forecasts, please take one". Dr Bel Kelland, you're here in town with a bunch of weather experts. Just last week we had a mini-tornado that took the roof off a building at the airport and grounded planes for four hours. And yet the forecast had been for fine weather all day. Shouldn't you all pack up and go home?'

Inwardly Bel cringed. Cale wasn't a proper news presenter; he was more like a vaudeville comedian. She didn't have time to swap banter with him – she needed to make some serious points. But if she handled it wrongly she'd just look prim and humourless. The director pointed to her. Time to reply.

'Jonny, I'd stick to the day job if I were you,' she said, her tone deliberately light. 'If you try to make it as a stand-up comic you're going to starve. But I agree with your underlying point. Weather forecasting *is* a joke at the moment. I could add many more examples – the ferry to Tasmania that sank in storms last month, the hailstorm in the middle of the Melbourne Carnival. All on days that were supposed to be fine. Weather forecasting is going wrong, and we need to ask why.'

Jonny replied, 'Why do we need weather forecasters at all?'

'For just the reasons you gave. Airlines need to know if their routes are going to be safe. So do shipping companies. Farmers and wine makers need to protect their crops.'

Jonny decided the discussion was getting too serious. He changed the subject. 'What about global warming? I always think it must be good news for somebody. People who make air conditioning?' He glanced at the camera and gave it a wink.

Bel cringed again. Jonny was obviously imagining the viewers at home chuckling appreciatively. She answered crisply, 'It will probably be very good news for people who build nuclear fallout shelters. When the weather goes loco, there's nowhere to hide. This planet was having tsunamis, hurricanes and ice ages long before mankind even rubbed two sticks together. But now we're taking this temperamental system and we're warming it up – and fast. Don't you think we should be more careful?'

Jonny moved on to another subject swiftly. 'So what is this I hear about weird US weather experiments?'

'What US experiments?' said Bel.

'As I was coming in this morning, I saw a lot of people with placards outside. They gave me this.' He got a crumpled sheet of paper out of his pocket and passed it to Bel. 'It says "Stop US experiments, come to the debate at 2 p.m. today". I ask again, what US experiments?'

Bel smoothed out the sheet of paper and glanced at it. It was a flyer from an environmental group called Oz Protectors, which she had never heard of. 'I've no idea,' she said. She looked at Jonny and smiled sweetly. 'But really, Jonny, I'm surprised. Someone gave you a piece of paper and they didn't want your autograph?'

The Oz Protectors – a group of five young people – were having a busy morning. They were putting leaflets through the doors of all the houses they could in Adelaide to encourage people to come to the public debate at the conference centre. Two members were in the town centre, handing out leaflets to passers-by. The other three – Timi, his girlfriend Amy, and her brother Joseph – were driving around the suburbs.

They'd started with the big, grand houses near the botanical gardens. As the three campaigners walked up long drives past sweeping lawns, they had met people leaving for work or collecting their mail. Some of them even chatted before taking a leaflet. Further away from the botanical gardens, the houses became smaller and more closely packed. The residents here were less friendly, but perhaps that was because Timi, Amy and Joseph were starting to look a bit frazzled in the heat. They had already been trudging up and down roads for two hours and Timi's battered red Golf didn't have air conditioning. Their yellow campaign T-shirts, which had started the morning crisp and fresh from the printers, were stained with sweat and smudged with red dust. Amy's long blonde dreadlock braids were curling up in the heat.

But still there was more to do. Timi parked his car in yet another street. Amy handed him a bottle of water and he drank a few mouthfuls before passing it to Joseph in the back seat and getting out of the car. The others joined him at the back door and loaded up their canvas satchels with leaflets before settting off again.

The houses here, built in the 1960s, were small and close together. They showed neglect: a lot of the white paintwork was peeling; the tiny front gardens were overgrown.

Timi stepped over an upturned rubbish bin to put a leaflet through a front door. The curtains in the window were closed, but as he lifted the flap of the letter box, a fat woman in a faded floral dress pulled the curtain aside and looked at him suspiciously.

As Timi stepped over the bin again, his phone rang. He didn't take it out, but peered into his trouser pocket to look at the screen. It showed that he'd received a text with a picture attachment. He'd get it out later to read; there was something about the area that made him uneasy about showing an expensive new phone.

Amy ran over to him from the other side of the

road, her dreadlocks bouncing. She looked excited.

'Wez just texted me. He managed to give one of our flyers to Jonny Cale just before he went on air!'

Timi's handsome Korean features wrinkled in disgust. 'I don't see what he's getting so excited about – Jonny Cale's an idiot.'

'Oi, you!'

They turned round to see Joseph hurdling a small white gate. He'd dropped his bag and was running in the direction of their car, shouting. Before he could reach it, the engine coughed into life and the car door slammed.

Timi and Amy gave chase but they were too slow. They stared in disbelief as the red hatchback roared off down the road and screeched round a corner, leaving a cloud of dust in its wake.

'Oh, brilliant!' shouted Amy. 'We're here trying to do some good, and a joyrider steals your blinking car.'

She heard a crunch behind her. When she looked round, Timi was kicking down a white picket fence.

'Tim!' she exclaimed. 'What are you doing?'

Joseph grabbed Timi by the arm and pulled him away. 'Hey, man, that doesn't help anyone.'

Timi swore at him in Korean, a furious sound like an animal snarling. His foot kicked out like a whiplash, splintering the white wood to smithereens. The violence of it made Joseph flinch.

'I'd just finished making the down payments on that car,' Timi snarled.

'Mate, it's not these people's fault,' said Joseph, looking at the ruined fence.

Timi whirled and grabbed him by the front of his T-shirt. 'No? They just look away – turn the other cheek, whether it's petty crime or the rape of the whole planet! It's *all* their bloody fault!'

He reached over the splintered fence, grabbed a garden gnome and dashed it to the ground. Plaster fragments shot everywhere. 'We're just wasting our time!' Timi was screaming. 'The world's going to hell and nobody wants to know.'

The noise was attracting attention. Amy saw grubby curtains twitching in the house next door. 'Timi, please – people can see . . .' she said quietly.

But Timi was in a blind rage. He didn't care whether people could see or not. He was caught up in his own world of fury.

* * *

Dodge took the hatchback around the streets at breakneck speed. That was good for about five minutes, but he soon got bored. The car had the reactions of a possum in a coma and it didn't even have air conditioning – he would have taken a tyre iron to it if he'd had the energy. But the two beers he'd drunk that morning, coupled with the heat, were making him feel a little sleepy. He drove to the municipal park, stopped and lay back in the car for a snooze.

He was awoken by a tap on the window. He saw a pale face and greasy dark hair. Snoopy. Dodge looked at his watch. Eleven a.m. That figured. Eleven was about the time Snoopy normally got up.

Dodge got out. 'Hey, Snoop, want to buy a car?' Snoopy was holding a can of lager. Dodge grabbed it and took a swig. With his other hand he clapped Snoopy on the shoulder. 'You can pay me later.'

Snoopy looked in through the window. 'Anything interesting in there?' He noticed the boxes of leaflets in the back. 'What're all these? And what's all this about?' He gestured at the windows, where there were several stickers. NUCLEAR POWER – NO THANKS! STOP

GLOBAL WARMING. OZ PROTECTORS FOR A HEALTHY PLANET.

Dodge went round to the rear and opened the door. He finished the beer, tossed the can into the car and lit a cigarette. With his free hand he picked up a couple of loose leaflets and touched the flame of his lighter to them. 'Yeah, stop global warming, eh?' he said to Snoopy, and sniggered.

'Hey,' said Snoopy, pointing to the flaming sheet of paper. 'Did you see that?'

'What?' Dodge replied. The flames reached his fingers and he dropped the burning paper, waving his fingers and blowing on them.

'The flame went kinda funny,' said Snoopy. 'Do it again.'

Dodge picked up another leaflet and lit it. The flames licked up the page, turning it black and crisp. Where they met the green Oz Protectors logo, they glowed bluey green.

Dodge grinned at Snoopy. 'Hey, pretty colours.'

'Told you,' said Snoopy.

He picked up some more of the leaflets, put them down on the parched grass and lit them with his lighter. They watched the flames intently, waiting for them to change colour when they reached the green printer's ink. When it happened, they grinned and took some more out of the box. A light breeze stirred the trees and fanned one of the flaming pages in Snoopy's hand. Curls of paper floated away across the grass like scraps of burning lace . . .

Chapter Four

Adelaide was surrounded on three sides by hills of vineyards. On the fourth side was the glittering blue ocean and thirty kilometres of white beach. Tram and train lines led from the beach to the city centre, which was laid out in rectangular blocks. Further out, in the residential areas, there were also parks and golf courses, a cemetery and a racecourse. Horses the size of ants were making their way around the white rails of the course.

It was the second time Ben had seen it all from the air and he was starting to get impatient. Kelly had said he could have a go at the controls, hadn't she?

'We've done the scenic tour,' he said. 'Surely it must be my turn to have a go at flying now?'

'Shh,' said Kelly. She checked something on the map on her knee and muttered to herself as if she was figuring out something important.

Ben suspected she was deliberately ignoring him. He leaned forward and pointed at the items on the instrument panel, one by one. 'That must be the altimeter . . . that's the airspeed indicator . . . radio . . . this is a global positioning system, fuel gauge, engine temperature, engine HT – that's the rev counter, isn't it? It's just like Microsoft Flight Simulator.'

Kelly made a contemptuous noise. 'Microsoft Flight Simulator? You sure know how to have fun. And don't imagine it's anything like real flying.' She raised the plane's nose and they climbed a little.

Ben sat back and folded his arms. 'Looks pretty much like a flight sim to me. In fact it's a lot less complicated than a Boeing Seven Eight Seven. Where's the artificial horizon?'

Kelly tapped a mark on the middle of the windscreen. 'There.'

She was pointing to a piece of black tape. For a

moment that took the wind out of Ben's sails. Surely she was joking? But there wasn't another artificial horizon on the instrument panel.

Kelly looked pleased at his reaction. 'Flying this is not like playing a computer game.' She moved her legs and looked down at the map on her lap again. Ben saw the pedals move on his side of the foot well. She was making little adjustments the whole time. It was fascinating.

He stretched his feet towards the pedals. 'What did you do just then?'

Kelly looked up from her map immediately. 'Don't touch those!' she snapped.

Ben pulled his feet back. 'So what do they do?'

'They're attached to the rudder.'

'And this joystick? That's steering, right?' He reached for the lever between the seats. 'Where's the throttle? Or is it on the joystick?'

Kelly batted his hand away from the controls. 'It's called the stick. A joystick's the thing on your Gamecube.' She made an irritable noise. 'Before you touch anything, I'm going to give you a rule. When I hand over to you, I will say, "You have control," and you say, "I have control." Otherwise you might think I'm flying the plane and I might think you're flying the plane and—'

Ben said: 'I have control,' and closed his fingers around the black rubber handle.

He thought Kelly might stop him but she didn't. He was now in charge of the plane. Butterflies danced in his stomach.

'Just push the stick forwards a tiny bit,' said Kelly, 'and keep an eye on the airspeed indicator here.'

Ben nudged the stick carefully forwards. The nose of the microlight pointed downwards. The racetrack below became visible through the front window and started to draw closer. He watched the airspeed indicator, watching the needle creep up. When it had gone up to about 50 knots, Kelly spoke again.

'OK, now level it off. Pull the stick back gently.'

Ben brought the nose slowly up again. The view of the racecourse disappeared and the windscreen was lined up with the horizon as before.

They were once again flying level.

Ben felt inordinately pleased with himself. He gave Kelly a wide grin.

'Now we'll try a turn. You can turn using the stick, but if you don't use the pedals as well you'll get too much yaw. Have a go at turning her right. Keep your right foot on the rudder pedal, but not too much.'

'How will I know when it's too much?'

Kelly tapped the horizon. 'Keep this as close to the middle as possible. Oh, and don't turn too sharply because we'll lose lift and airspeed.'

Ben looked around at the controls. 'Will we need the throttle? Where is it, by the way?'

'Forget about the throttle,' said Kelly firmly. 'Just turn using the stick and pedals.'

Ben pushed the stick away from him and pushed his foot gently on the pedal.

The microlight turned. This was easy.

Suddenly Ben's stomach seemed to leave his body, making for the top of the craft. He let go of the controls.

The plane was dropping out of the sky.

The map flew off Kelly's lap and over her shoulder, like a trapped seagull. She snatched it back and, with her other hand, grabbed the stick. 'You idiot!' she yelled. 'What did you do?!'

Just as suddenly, the plane flew smoothly again. But the altimeter said they had fallen a hundred feet.

Ben was white. He was gripping the seat so hard his fingers hurt. 'I didn't do anything. It just went by itself.'

The respite was short-lived. The plane started to jump up and down, like a boat on choppy water. Kelly tried to control it with the stick and the pedals. She pointed the nose upwards and the engine roared as she tried to regain the height they had lost.

But at least it seemed to be under control again. Ben's stomach was calming down. He even felt able to make a joke.

'When do we get to loop the loop—?'

His words ended in a strangled sound. The plane dropped again, like an elevator plummeting with a snapped cable. Ben's buttocks lifted off the seat. If he hadn't had the seat belt on he'd have gone clean through the roof. He was paralysed with fear, only just able to hold on.

Kelly was struggling with the controls. The engine above them seemed to be screaming. Ben caught a glimpse of the instruments. They were doing crazy things, the needles swinging from side to side.

Then the bright blue sky around the cockpit went dark, and Ben realized he could smell smoke.

Something was burning.

Was the microlight on fire? He looked behind and above. Where was the smell coming from?

The windscreen cleared again, the smoke disappeared and they soared away into blue sky. Kelly watched the dials with fierce concentration, making adjustments. Ben gripped the seat, dreading it happening again.

But the craft was flying calmly now. And he could no longer smell smoke.

Kelly relaxed and unclosed her fingers from around the stick. She was breathing hard, like she had been running.

Ben let go of the seat again. 'I didn't do that, did I?'

Kelly shook her head. 'You couldn't do something like that even if you were flying in boxing gloves. There must be something outside that did it.'

Ben craned around in his seat to see where the smoke had come from. A black plume rose from the park below. Bright orange flames flickered through the tinder-dry trees, consuming them one after the other as though they were no more substantial than twigs. Ben had never seen anything like it.

Kelly was peering out of the other side. 'We caught the thermals from that fire. It must be giving off heat like a furnace.'

The park adjoined a street of houses and the fire was eating through the trees like lightning. Soon it would run out of trees, and the next thing in its path was the row of houses.

'Oh my gosh,' said Kelly. 'That looks really out of control. Call nine-one-one.'

Ben slid his phone out of his pocket. He knew she meant the emergency services – 999 in the UK. 'Actually,' he said, 'here it's treble-zero.'

Wanasri Kongprapoon had only finished her firefighter training the previous week. She had signed in for her first shift and was just stashing her kit in her new locker when the call came in. The trees in the municipal park near the cemetery were on fire. Now she was in the cab of Engine 33, craning her neck out of the window to look at the pall of smoke on the hill.

In the cab with her were her new team-mates, whom she had met for the first time that morning: Petra Wardell, the driver and team leader, and fire-fighters Andy Delmonte and Darren Beogh.

The crew hadn't exactly looked thrilled when they were introduced to their new colleague. Wanasri's family were from Thailand, and although she was tall, her build was slight. Andy, Darren and Petra were all big Australians with broad shoulders. Andy was in his forties and heavy-set. Wanasri could see what was going through their minds as they were introduced. What use will someone so small be as a firefighter?

Now they might have to trust her with their lives, and she had to trust in them. Today, Wanasri had a lot to prove.

The smoke was drifting towards them. All the crew coughed as it caught at the back of their throats. There was no smell like it. Wanasri recognized the resiny tang of burning eucalyptus. It sent a surge of adrenaline pumping through her veins. She felt ready for anything, like a soldier psyched up for combat.

Ahead was a big wooden fence. The tall trees

behind it were blazing, sending orange flames shooting ten metres into the sky.

The engine stopped beside a big house clad in white weatherboard. This would be their front line – the territory they had to protect. If they couldn't put out the burning trees, the fire would spread to the house and it would go up like kindling . . .

Wanasri jumped smartly out of the cab, putting her yellow helmet on. She fastened the catch under her chin and pulled the visor down as the heat hit her like a furnace. Andy and Darren had already begun unwinding the hose lines and Petra grabbed one, ran in and started to play the water into the flames.

Wanasri picked up a line too. The metal nozzle was heavy in her hands. The water started to course down inside it, making it move like a live snake. She looked towards the fire as she had done hundreds of times in training – and froze. This was a real fire, not a practice. Somebody's home was under threat.

Darren dragged a hose past her and shouted, 'What are you doing? Get stuck in!'

That kick-started something in Wanasri's brain. There was a gap in the line, waiting for her. She ran in.

Her firefighting career had well and truly started.

She had never frozen like that in training. She didn't know what had come over her, but she resolved that it would never happen again.

The water poured out of the hoses in white arcs. When it hit the burning columns of vegetation it turned into steam. The eucalyptus trees were rich in oils and burned particularly well. The heat rose, creating thermal currents, sucking flaming fragments into the air. They landed on other trees and set them alight. As fast as one tree was put out, another was catching.

Wanasri's team was driving the fire away from the house. Meanwhile another team attacked it from the other side of the fence, and a third crew was drenching the walls and roof of the house in case a burning branch came its way.

Wanasri had seen house fires in training, both as simulations and in films illustrating lectures. She had those pictures in her mind now. You could always see what it had been like before the fire: the outlines of paintings or mirrors on the walls; the sofas reduced to metal frames after the cushions had been gobbled up by the flames. Worse still were the items that were irreplaceable: the fragments of photos, the books, the videotapes. The devastation was obscene. That was what would happen to this house in front of her if she failed.

Wanasri's arms soon ached with the strain of holding the nozzle. Her turnout gear – as they called the heavy protective suits and boots – felt stiff and new, and stiflingly heavy. The heat was so intense it felt like it would crack her face. It made her think of a sausage skin bursting on a barbecue. But still she carried on. She blasted the flames with water and followed up every little orange tongue she could see. She would protect that house with every last breath in her body.

They carried on soaking the charred fence; the trees behind it had been reduced to black skeletons.

Finally Wanasri felt the hose sag in her hands. The hiss of the water stopped. For a moment the site fell silent. Every member of the three teams was on tenterhooks. Was the fire out?

Steam made a grey cloud around the house. Water dripped off the eaves. The sunlight picked out droplets on the pink and yellow tricycle in the front garden.

The grass and the paved drive were littered with burned twigs and rubbish that had fallen out of the sky. Any one of them could have set the house ablaze.

But none of it was burning any longer.

A moment ago Wanasri had felt exhausted. Now, as she coiled up her hose, she was on top of the world. They had done it. They had saved somebody's home.

A white police 4x4 pulled up between the red engines. Two officers climbed out, pulling yellow safety vests on over their uniforms.

One of them called to Petra, who was closing the water valves on the truck. 'Is it all out?'

Petra nodded. 'It's all yours.'

A gate opened in the charred fence. A fireman from one of the other crews stepped through and beckoned to the policemen. 'Officer, I think you should come and see this. Looks like this fire was started deliberately.'

Chapter Five

Kelly pushed open the glass doors of the flying club. Ben followed her in. The air conditioning was a welcome relief from the heat outside. Ben found it was no longer a novelty to be sweltering hot in the middle of February.

When they phoned the police to report the fire they were told they'd be asked to give a statement, so Kelly had cut their flight short and brought them back.

The foyer of the club was like a hotel: palm trees, an atrium and a few big canvases of aboriginal art. At the front desk was a young male receptionist in an open-necked shirt that showed off a tan. As soon as

Kelly saw him, her behaviour changed. She checked her flying suit, which was once again knotted like a jumper around her hips, took off the orange baseball cap and shook her blonde hair free. Then she went up to the desk. Ben tagged along, feeling rather embarrassed.

Kelly leaned on the counter and gave the receptionist her most dazzling Texan smile. 'Hi – I'm expecting a visitor. A police officer. My name's Kelly Kurtis.'

The receptionist consulted a large diary beside the switchboard. 'They haven't arrived yet, Miss Kurtis,' he said. 'Actually, hang on a sec. A parcel came for you.' He turned round and picked up a large box that was resting against the desk. It was the size of a tea chest.

'Oh, that was quick,' said Kelly. She smiled again. 'I'm afraid I've been shopping.'

'Is that right?' said the receptionist. 'Looks a bit big to be shoes.'

Kelly shook her head and gave him an enigmatic look. 'It's a power chute.'

'What's a power chute?' asked Ben.

Kelly glared at him. It was a look that said, *Children should be seen and not heard.* Then she turned her attention back to the receptionist, hooked her phone out of her trouser pocket and showed him the picture on her start-up page. 'That's me and some friends power chuting in Wyoming.'

The receptionist looked at it, then nodded. 'Oh, those. We've got a couple of members who do that off the runway. They must be mad.'

Ben could see Kelly took the remark as a compliment to her bravery. 'You've got to know what you're doing,' she said. 'You have to read the air currents, like a sailor reading the sea.' She made to put the phone away.

'Can I see?' said Ben.

Kelly gave him the phone just to keep him quiet, then started to lift the box down. 'I don't know how I'm going to get this out to my Jeep,' she said, and gave the receptionist an appealing smile.

Meanwhile Ben was fascinated by the picture. It showed Kelly dangling under a red and pink striped parachute with an engine strapped to her back. 'Wow,' he said. 'What is that thing?'

The receptionist answered him. 'You put this engine on your back, then you clip on a parachute and buzz about in the air like a motorized maybug. You've got to be crackers, I reckon.'

Ben looked at the box that Kelly was trying to lift onto the floor. 'And that's all in there? Can I see?'

Kelly ignored him, but the receptionist answered, 'You can buy those things in town. There's an outdoor shop that stocks them.' He noticed that someone had arrived at the other end of the counter. 'Excuse me.'

Ben looked at Kelly. 'I'll put the box in the car for you if you let me look at the chute later.'

Kelly gave him an irritated look and lifted the box easily off the counter.

Suit yourself, thought Ben. Sorry I'm not twenty-two years old.

'Miss Kurtis,' said the receptionist. 'Your visitor is just parking now. You can use the manager's office if you need some privacy. Would you like me to look after your parcel for you?'

The policeman took off his cap and put it on the desk. The cap was white, with an intricate badge and a black peak which was so highly polished it showed a reflection of the fan rotating in the ceiling. His radio, clipped to a shoulder strap, made quiet crackles as it picked up the transmissions of other officers out on patrol. He sat down at the desk in the manager's office, keys and handcuffs jangling at his belt.

'Sorry to interrupt your plans,' he said. 'I won't take up too much of your time.' He took a notebook and pen out of his breast pocket. 'Can you tell me briefly what you saw when you reported the fire?'

Ben and Kelly pulled up chairs. Kelly shrugged as she sat down. 'We didn't see much really. It was burning quite well by the time we spotted it.'

'You didn't see any suspicious characters?'

'Officer,' said Kelly, 'we were a thousand feet up.' There was a poster on the wall of the airfield, showing the ground as photographed from a plane. A Cessna on the ground was just about visible as a small white arrow on a two-inch strip of black runway. She pointed to it. 'It all looks like that. You can't see what people are doing.'

The police officer looked at the poster and put his pen down. 'I thought that's what you might say. It's just that we have strong reasons to believe the fire was arson. As you were the people who alerted the authorities, you're officially regarded as witnesses and so we have to question you. There is one piece of evidence I'd like you to look at. Again, I don't suppose you can tell me anything, but I'm asking just in case.' He took a sheet of paper out of his notebook, unfolded it and handed it to Ben and Kelly.

It was a photocopy of a leaflet. The bottom part had been burned.

'A stack of these leaflets was found at the scene of the fire. If we knew who produced them we might be closer to finding our arsonist.'

Kelly glanced at the leaflet, then saw something that made her take notice. She read it out: ' "Stop secret US experiments" – what's all this about?' She scan-read the rest of the text and made a contemptuous noise. 'Typical environmental scaremongering. They always make Americans out to be the bad guys.' She handed the leaflet to Ben. 'Your mom might know who these retards are.'

Ben read the leaflet. The contents were actually quite weird.

Not far from Adelaide, in the Great Victoria Desert near Coober Pedy, the American military built a listening station a couple of years ago. Ever since then, the people of Coober Pedy have been stricken by a number of strange sicknesses. Depression, skin diseases, strange allergies and migraines have all doubled in the Coober Pedy population. Not only that, but farm animals have been becoming ill, for reasons that vets are unable to explain. We want to know what goes on there. Are they polluting the water? The atmosphere? Are they releasing radiation or biological particles? This American-built listening station is counted as US soil. They do not have to stick to our laws – the laws that protect the environment and the people who live and work there. They do not have to declare what goes on there. Worse, if these sicknesses travel, could Adelaide—

The rest was charred and unreadable. But after reading it, the sound of the police officer's radio crackling away in the background seemed quite eerie.

'Son, why might your mother know about this leaflet?'

'She's an environmental scientist,' Ben said. 'Her name's Dr Bel Kelland and she's speaking at the conference centre today.'

The officer passed Ben his notebook and pen. 'Can you give me her contact details?'

Ben wrote down his mum's mobile number and passed the pad back. 'I doubt she'd know these people. She deals with more serious stuff: tsunamis and things. Governments come to her for advice. She doesn't hang around with fringe groups and nutters.'

Kelly leaned back in her chair, her arms folded. 'Officer, do you really think the fire was started deliberately?'

'Miss, we get one or two deliberate fires in Adelaide every month. There's a small proportion of the population who like to see things burn.' The officer put his pen and notepad away.

'Why would environmental protestors start a fire?' asked Ben. 'That's not very green, is it?'

The police officer put his hat back on. 'I admit it seems strange.'

The radio on his shoulder crackled and this time it was louder. '*Fire on Veale Gardens. Engines have been dispatched. Fire investigation officers, stand by.'*

He sighed. 'That's another fire. Thanks for your time. If either of you folks remember anything later on, give the station a call. Keep that leaflet, and if you see your mum before I do, would you show it to her?'

Ben nodded.

As soon as the officer had gone, Kelly looked at her watch. 'You're probably hungry. We should go to the cafeteria.'

Ben didn't feel remotely interested in food. 'I only got about two minutes' flying,' he protested. 'I thought I was going to get a proper lesson.'

'It's quite strenuous,' said Kelly. 'Two minutes is a lot of time to concentrate if you're only thirteen.' She started to walk towards the cafeteria.

Ben fumed. He wasn't going to let her brush him off like that. He caught up with her and spoke in a low voice. 'If you take me up again and give me a proper lesson I'll go and amuse myself this afternoon so you can chat up George on reception.'

Kelly stopped in her tracks. She looked at him, astonished. Her voice came out as an incredulous whisper. 'How do you know he's called George?'

'His records were on the desk in the manager's office. I know other things about him too, which I might tell you later.' Ben put on a pleasant smile and indicated the direction of the front door. 'Shall we go for a spin?'

Chapter Six

Wanasri was having a busy day. Engine 33 had been called to a two-storey warehouse on the edge of town. Two teams were already there, playing hoses over the flames, but the fire was licking through the walls and the floors. A giant plume of black smoke hung in the air, blotting out the sun. Nearby, in the drive of the warehouse next door, a group of twenty or more people had gathered, watching the fire with expressions of dismay. A few of them were probably bystanders, but the rest were employees evacuated from the building.

As Wanasri jumped down from the truck, she saw

three firefighters in breathing masks coming out of the building. Their turnout gear was glistening wet and they were moving slowly, as though their clothes were very heavy. She had seen that distinctive walk before; it meant the heat was taking its toll. Inside the warehouse must be very hot – much hotter than the fire they had just been to.

Petra gave Wanasri and the others a pep talk as they pulled on their gear. 'The other crews have cleared the ground floor. You've got to check the top floor. The guys think the manager is up there as he's the only one unaccounted for. The fire's been knocked back to the ground floor, so you'll have to be quick. Take breathing gear.' She opened a hatch at the side of the red truck. Backpacks and masks were hanging there ready on pegs.

Wanasri picked up a breathing pack and shrugged it over her bony shoulders onto her back.

Andy was watching her as she did up the fastening. 'Is this your first time inside?'

Wanasri guessed Andy was wondering if she would freeze again. 'Yes,' she said. 'I'll be OK.' She took down a mask, wiped the visor clean and pulled it over her head. It smelled of rubber and smoke. She took a few moments to acclimatize. She hated wearing the mask. You couldn't see very well through the goggles and it stopped you hearing anything but your own breathing. And it was always unsettling to put one on and breathe the smell of the previous fire. It always made Wanasri wonder, How had that one turned out?

Darren clapped her on the back. 'Come on, let's go!'

Wanasri pulled her helmet on, grabbed a small extinguisher and ran with them up the metal fire escape on the outside of the building. Darren jemmied open the fire door with a crowbar and they were in.

The interior of the building was black with smoke. The heat was like opening an oven door.

Although the Engine 33 crew carried small extinguishers, it wasn't their job now to put out flames. Wanasri, Petra, Darren and Andy would have to rely on the firefighters outside to do that.

Petra switched on her torch and touched Darren on the shoulder. That was the signal to pair off. They started to walk carefully into the darkened warehouse.

The smoke swallowed them up. They became invisible, except for flashes of torchlight glancing on glowing yellow bands.

Wanasri and Andy set off towards the right-hand side of the building. They stayed close together, walking slowly. Wanasri's amplified breathing sucked and rasped in her ears. Her torch turned the smoke into glowing fog. They had to move by feel, which made the search process agonizingly slow. That was why they needed four people to search one floor in a warehouse.

Along the middle of the room, a series of metal shelves was stacked with surfboards. The paint was peeling in the heat. Wanasri noted that and was glad of her mask. She was a surfer herself and knew the materials in the boards could combust and give off poisonous fumes.

She noticed that the fire was licking along the skirting boards. Were her eyes getting used to the gloom, or was the fire on the floor below burning harder? At this rate, it wouldn't be long before the walls up here caught as well.

Wanasri took another step and felt something give

under her feet. Too late, she registered what was happening. The floorboards had given way, and she was crashing through! Beyond her feet was a hungry mass of flames.

She was falling into them—

Suddenly something stopped her. As she was dragged back, she looked round in shock. Andy had managed to catch the straps of her airpack, and he hauled her back onto her feet. Her breath roared inside her respirator. Below, the flames burned and crackled. If she had fallen through she would have been trapped down there.

She'd had a narrow escape.

There was no time now to think about that, though. She still had a job to do. She tore her gaze away from the flames that had so nearly claimed her and continued her search, stepping even more carefully through the building.

She saw movement ahead, a flash of fluorescent jacket in her torchlight. Petra was bending over something on the floor, then she straightened up slowly. Over her shoulder was a limp figure wearing a breathing mask.

They had found the manager. And he was alive.

Wanasri went to help Petra carry him down.

Bel was in the foyer waiting for Major Kurtis. He had gone out to post a birthday card to his wife. Surely that shouldn't take long? She looked at her watch. He'd been gone for ten minutes, even though he was supposed to be on the panel debating weather forecasting technology and it was starting in barely five minutes. She needed to brief him, but they were fast running out of time.

Outside was a group of environmental campaigners with placards. They had been gathering since early that morning, eager to join in the public debate later in the afternoon. Some of them wore T-shirts from old Fragile Earth campaigns. Good for you, thought Bel.

Others carried placards. She saw: WHAT REALLY CAUSED THE OZONE LAYER HOLE? And STOP SECRET US EXPERIMENTS.

That one must be from the mysterious Oz Protectors who had leafleted Jonny Cale that morning. If she got time before the public debate, she'd go and chat to them and find out what their issues were.

Bel looked at her watch. In fact, if the major didn't hurry up and come back, maybe she'd haul the campaigners in to take his place.

When she looked back at the door, the campaigners' placards had moved. Before, they had been spread out in a line; now they were bunched together around something, and there was shouting.

The conference centre security guard pulled open the door and went outside. Curious, Bel followed him.

Before she even got as far as the door, the guard was coming back. He had a sheltering arm around Major Kurtis and was barging protestors out of the way as he escorted him back into the foyer.

'What happened to you?' said Bel.

'The rent-a-mob guys collared me.' The major had an Oz Protectors leaflet in his hand. He crumpled it into a ball and dropped it into the rubbish bin. 'They see the uniform and they all think the worst.'

Bel folded her arms. 'Well, that's not entirely surprising, is it? The United States has the worst record on green issues. These people protest because they care, and thank God they do.'

'I'm not arguing with that,' said the major, still clearly rattled by his encounter with the protestors. 'But not every bad thing that happens in the world is the fault of the US, you know.'

Bel stepped aside to let a group of delegates go through into the auditorium. 'Time's getting on, we need to talk about this debate. We've had to change the other speaker . . . Ah, here he is.' She waved, and a figure walking down the stairs waved back and started walking towards them. 'Dr Yamanouchi?'

The elderly man in a rumpled corduroy suit, his black hair threaded with grey, was about to greet Bel when his eyes opened wide with surprise.

'Brad Kurtis. I didn't recognize you at first.'

'Dr Yamanouchi,' replied the major. 'How are you?'

'Do you two know each other?' said Bel.

'Dr Yamanouchi was my tutor at Harvard,' replied the major.

The doctor looked at the major again, shaking his head. 'You know, the last thing I would have expected was to see you in a military uniform.'

The major gave Dr Yamanouchi a broad Texan smile. 'It's not what I imagined myself doing twenty years ago, but it's worked out quite well.'

'Don't tell me you're a soldier,' said the doctor. 'You must have sold them one of your vastly impractical schemes.'

Bel was interested. 'His schemes?'

Major Kurtis smoothed his hand over his cropped hair. 'My strength was theoretical research. Whereas Dr Yamanouchi thought I should be finding new ways to analyse rainfall.'

'Yes, I still remember Brad going on about weather control. He talked about nothing else for months. You had your head in the clouds in those days.'

Major Kurtis gave a forced laugh. 'Well, at least I've moved on from that. Those corduroy trousers look like the same ones you used to wear twenty years ago.'

Bel put her hands up to call for silence. 'Time out, guys. Save it for in there. If you two argue like that on the stage we're going to have a great debate. Let's get this show on the road.'

As Bel shepherded them into the auditorium, she heard a rapping noise on the window outside.

She turned and saw one of the campaigners waving. He pressed a placard up against the window and rapped on the glass again, as if trying to reinforce its message:

STOP SECRET US EXPERIMENTS.

Chapter Seven

Ben was up in the microlight again. Down below were the gentle hills and valleys of the vineyards. Kelly had planned a flight path that steered well clear of the fire area.

And Ben had control.

Kelly's voice came through on his headset. 'Let's practise those turns. Remember, don't just use the stick, use the pedals as well. Don't turn too sharply because you'll lose airspeed. Feel what the craft is doing by watching your horizon.'

Ben executed a flawless turn. The horizon barely tilted.

'Very good,' said Kelly. 'Now try the other way.'

Ben had a little think about what each hand and leg had to do, then turned the craft expertly left. Whatever Kelly might say, it wasn't that different from flight sims on the PC.

'Always make sure you come back to level after you've turned; don't just assume you have. We try to keep the plane as level as possible. Now tell me your height.'

She certainly was giving him a thorough lesson. Ben took a moment to locate the altimeter. 'Eleven hundred feet.'

'That's getting a bit low. We want to be no lower than a thousand feet unless we're coming in to land. We prefer to be at fifteen hundred to two thousand feet, because that gives us a bit of leeway in case we drift down or the weather conditions take us by surprise. So gently point the nose upwards and open the throttle – that's the stick on your left-hand side by the door. Pull it up to increase the revs.'

Ben grasped the throttle. With his right hand he raised the nose and with the left he pulled the throttle lever up. The engine became louder. He felt it pull harder. The plane began to climb.

'Watch the horizon,' said Kelly. 'You don't want to go too steeply. Take her steadily.' She peered out of the window.

'What's wrong?' said Ben. 'Have we dropped something?'

'I'm keeping an eye on the ground. In case we have to ditch.'

'Why would we want to ditch?'

'It's just something you always have to watch out for. You should be doing it really.'

Ben looked at the altimeter. 'We're at fifteen hundred feet now.'

'That'll do. Ease off the throttle and let the nose come level.'

Ben did as he was told. The engine became quieter. He sat back, took his hands and feet off the controls and let the plane cruise.

But Kelly didn't think his job was done. 'What's your bearing? Are we still on course or have we drifted?'

Ben checked the compass. 'Heading south-west. Is that correct?'

'Yes, that's fine.' Kelly looked out of the window again. Ben wished she wouldn't keep doing that.

'Look at what's below us,' said Kelly's voice in his headphones.

Ben looked out of the side window. Below them was a vineyard, a rolling tapestry of golden leaves sprinkled with purple. 'Trees and stuff,' he said.

'And what else?'

'A big hill.' He straightened up again. Looking down like that made him feel a bit queasy.

'What height are you at?' said Kelly.

He gave Kelly a smile. 'Don't worry, we'll get over the hill.'

'Look at the altimeter,' said Kelly.

Ben suspected she was doing this to bug him so that he'd be grateful when the lesson was over. 'I told you a moment ago, we're at fifteen hundred feet. And I haven't changed anything. So we're still at fifteen hundred feet.'

'Just look at the darned instruments.'

Ben pointed to the altimeter as if to emphasize that he was right. And got a surprise. 'Oh. It says seventeen hundred feet.'

'Right, mister vidgame pilot. You get thermals from hills and woods, and they take you up or down without you realizing it. You need to adjust to fifteen hundred feet again. And then, when we're over the ridge, check the thermals haven't taken us down. And that we're still on course.'

'Is there anything else you want me to do at the same time?' said Ben. His brain hurt.

'You wanted to learn to fly – well, I'm teaching you. You don't just sit here and put your feet up, or fix yourself a cup of coffee. And by the way, you're getting off lightly. You should also be checking the map, the amount of fuel you have left and how long you've been up. Oh, and as I said, keep an eye out for likely landing sites.'

As Ben made the adjustments, Kelly sat back, resting her elbow along the window and drumming her fingers. 'You know, I once had to land a microlight on the West Seattle Bridge as part of a display. Although the bridge was straight and wide enough, there were air currents because of the river. It was a real test of skill. You had to feel what the plane was doing, and if you took your eye off the ball for just a moment—'

'Save it for when you need to impress George,' said
Ben.

The house was on a hill. A two-storey building over-
looking the woods on one side and the Adelaide
botanical gardens on the other, it was now shrouded
in smoke and steam as thick as a sea fog. The woods
were on fire and three crews were trying to stop the
flames reaching the house. Engine 33 was one of
them.

The fire was getting closer. Wanasri couldn't see it,
but she could feel the temperature rising with every
minute she stood there, directing her hose into the
dense cloud. Even though she was wearing goggles,
her nose was running and her eyes were watering.
Andy, Petra and Darren were standing in a row next
to her.

Saving the house was top priority, and if they failed,
the consequences could be very serious. The fire
would spread to the botanical gardens next door. Its
fifty acres of unusual plants and trees were all tinder-
dry in the heat. And beyond the botanical gardens lay
a closely packed residential estate.

Saving this house would save all of them.

Suddenly the fire hose went limp in Wanasri's hands.

She whirled round. What had happened? They had lost water pressure. Andy was running back to the engine to deal with it.

When she looked back, flames were rolling towards her fast like a big orange wave. Without the hoses they couldn't keep it back. It was too late to run – the flames were already on top of her. Fire licked against her mask, blinding her. The heat seared her, even through the heavy suit. She dived to the ground.

She heard rather than felt the water falling on her. When she looked up, Darren was hosing her down. Andy must have got the water back on. Just in time.

Wanasri got to her feet and gave Darren a thumbs-up. The fire retardant in her turnout gear had saved her from serious burns. But that didn't mean it didn't sting.

She retrieved her hose and opened the nozzle again. The water came through, straight and true, and she aimed it into the woods. She couldn't see anything because of the smoke, but she remembered this from her training. So long as she wasn't seeing flames, it was under control.

After a few minutes the heat was easing. The smoke thinned out to reveal a blackened mass of twisted branches. Wanasri turned her hose off to give the steam time to settle. Then they would be able to see if the fire really was out. She turned round.

And saw a flicker inside the house.

She yelled at the top of her voice, 'Fire inside!' She ran across the lawn, up onto the sun deck and in through the French windows. The hose snaked along behind her. Her eyes searched from left to right, up and down – where was that flame?

Petra's boots thudded onto the decking behind her. 'Where is it?'

Wanasri peered through the smears on her goggles. She couldn't see.

Petra suddenly called out. 'There!' She pushed past the sofa then stopped. 'I've lost it again.' Sometimes chasing a stray flame around a house was like trying to catch a wild bird. 'Darn you,' muttered Petra, looking around the skirting board. 'Come on out.'

Then Wanasri spotted it. She went towards the corner of the room – and realized it was only the amber LED on a computer monitor, flashing every few seconds to show it was on standby. 'False alarm,' she called. She reached out her gloved hand and switched it off, just to be sure.

Petra walked back to the French windows. Darren and Andy were coming in, portable extinguishers in each hand. Petra chucked her hose out onto the lawn and took an extinguisher from Darren. Wanasri did likewise.

Now they had to check over the rest of the house. The fire had sent a lot of burning debris into the air and some of it might have blown in. The Engine 33 crew searched upstairs. Other crews came in and took the ground floor. Cupboards were opened, cushions were turned over, rugs were shaken, furniture was moved – all in case a stray spark was smouldering away unseen in a corner.

Upstairs, the house was clear. Wanasri led the way down to the ground floor. The other fire crews were congregating in the hall. The limewashed floorboards were criss-crossed with wet black footprints.

'All clear down here,' said a member of another crew as he pulled off his helmet.

Wanasri felt a broad smile breaking across her face. Cheers and whistles rose around her. They had saved this house – and the botanical gardens, and the housing estate. She saw a gloved hand stretched out to her. She slapped it enthusiastically. High fives took the place of words. Her first day. She felt bone-weary but prouder than she had ever been.

Outside, the air smelled of damp smoke. But it was a good smoky smell – the smell of plain old burned wood, not the acrid, chemical fumes of a house fire.

The hoses were wound away, the ladders stowed, and the crews departed for their stations.

Sitting high up in the cab of Engine 33 between Andy and Darren, with Petra at the wheel, Wanasri could see over the wall of the botanical gardens. It was a calming space with rolling lawns and beautiful manicured trees.

'You're having a hell of an initiation,' said Petra to Wanasri. 'It's not usually like this. There must be some mischief-makers about.'

Darren leaned across Wanasri. 'Talking of initiation – Andy, get her helmet off.'

Andy grinned and unclipped Wanasri's chin harness. Darren lifted her helmet away. Petra, at the wheel, chuckled.

Wanasri regarded them with big, suspicious eyes. 'What are you guys doing?'

Darren slid his fingers over the grime on her helmet. It left two rows of clean yellow streaks.

'Hold her still, Andy,' said Darren.

Andy pinned her arms by her sides.

Darren extended his sooty fingers towards her face.

Wanasri realized what he was going to do. 'No!' she squealed and tried to squirm away. But with Andy's bulk squashed against her there was nowhere to go. Darren, grinning, drew on her face with the sooty fingers.

As soon as Andy released her, she pulled down the flap of the sun visor and inspected the damage in the mirror. Darren had drawn tiger stripes across her forehead and cheeks.

'I'll get you back,' growled Wanasri, secretly pleased she had been so clearly accepted by the crew.

Petra braked at a junction and looked both ways before easing the big engine through a ninety-degree turn. 'Hey,' she noted, 'it's getting kinda windy out there. Look at those trees.'

The other crew members had been so busy giving Wanasri her initiation stripes that they hadn't been paying much attention to what was going on outside. The tall eucalyptus trees along the road were waving hard, as though someone was shaking them. So were the aerials and satellite dishes on the roofs of the houses. Dustbins fell over and their contents were snatched away in a whirling storm.

Darren pointed along the road. 'Hey, see that smoke over there?'

At the end of the road, a black plume of smoke rose into the sky. It was slanting at forty-five degrees, blown by the wind.

Instantly the mood in the truck turned serious. It was as though someone had flipped a switch. The crew were back on duty.

Petra put the siren on and pressed the accelerator to the floor.

Darren spoke into the radio. 'Control, this is Engine

Thirty-three. We're going to investigate smoke on Oak Street. We might need back-up.'

The wheel jiggled from side to side in Petra's hands. She fought to keep it straight. 'That is some cross-wind. The truck's steering like a supermarket trolley.'

Wanasri buckled her helmet back on.

When they reached Oak Street, Petra braked, skidding, and the truck pulled up beside a big corrugated-iron fence. They had barely come to a halt before Andy jumped out. He ran over to the gate and started to pull it open. Then he snatched his hand back with a yell.

'It's hot!'

Darren brought over the bolt cutters. He hooked them around the handle on the door and yanked the gate open.

Intense heat slammed into them like a wall. With the heat came a choking smell of burning rubber. They were in a scrap merchant's yard. A mountain of tyres lay in one corner, heaped up against the iron fence, and they were on fire. The wind was fanning the flames, throwing black smoke and burning scraps of rubber into the air. That was why the blaze had looked small from a distance. The high wind was whipping the smoke away, diluting it. But that same wind was also carrying the burning scraps in a wide arc over the houses.

Petra screamed into her radio. 'Need major back-up on Oak Street *now*! Code Red! *Code Red*!'

Chapter Eight

Ben thought he was doing pretty well. He was flying big loops and figures of eight and learning to ride the air currents over the hills and valleys of the vineyards. He was even wondering if Kelly might let him try a landing.

Suddenly the plane started going sideways. It felt as though a giant hand was pushing the fuselage.

Kelly was aware of it immediately. She looked up from the map on her lap. 'Jeez, where did that wind come from? Give me control.'

'You've got it.' Ben was relieved to hand over to her. He tucked his feet under the seat, let her take the stick and sat back. He felt the pedals move up and down as she tried to compensate for the wind. The engine roared above his head as Kelly opened the throttle.

He relaxed. Flying was actually quite tiring. There was so much to think about. It felt good to let Kelly worry about it for a while.

His relief didn't last for long. Despite everything Kelly was doing, the microlight was still drifting off course. He could see her tugging the stick from side to side, her knees going up and down as she worked the pedals furiously. He could see the cables that ran through the cockpit to the rudder sawing backwards and forwards. But they were having no effect. The engine was straining but it couldn't push them forwards. The craft was being pitched sideways like a paper boat.

Sitting in a fragile bubble 1500 feet above the ground was a bad place to be when things started to go wrong. Ben expected any moment to feel a great bang and see a wing snap off and tumble past the cockpit.

Kelly managed to get the nose down, and they started losing altitude.

Ben noticed the altimeter. 'Kelly, we're at nine hundred feet.'

Kelly stuck her head out of the window but her voice still carried on in his headset. 'I know. I'm going to land.'

Ben looked out of the window. They lost height very quickly. The rows of vines, which were visible only as stripes in the landscape at cruising altitude, enlarged into distinct hedges. Ben was convinced he could see the individual leaves. They were being ruffled in a strong wind. In between the hedgerows were wide avenues of bare red earth.

Kelly lined up on one of the avenues and pointed the nose towards the ground. She closed down the throttle. The engine noise lowered, like a singer humming down through a scale. Ben felt the plane lose airspeed. He could make out more details on the ground now. Wooden poles and netting holding up the vines. The herringbone marks where tractors had driven down the avenue.

The microlight seemed to hop sideways in the air. Kelly pumped her feet up and down on the pedals. Her voice came through on the headset, muttering through gritted teeth. 'Don't you dare . . .'

The nose lifted. Ben felt a bump. For a moment he thought what he had been dreading had happened; that something had snapped off. Then there was a bump at the front as well. That was the wheels touching down.

Above their heads, the engine stopped. Kelly squeezed the brake hard. Ben could feel the friction as the brakes bit into the wheels, and every jolt and rut in the track jarred him. It was like taking a sports car over a hundred speed bumps at full tilt. But he was very grateful to be back on the ground.

The plane slewed to a halt on the dusty track, its tail poking into a row of vines.

'We'll wait it out here,' said Kelly. 'We're too small and light to make any headway in a wind like that.' She secured the brake with the strip of Velcro, turned off all the systems and undid her seat belt.

Ben stepped out the other side, easing the stiffness in his limbs. The dusty ground felt rock hard under his feet, completely dried out after months of drought. Without the breeze they felt when flying, the heat was stifling. The flying suits stuck to their skin. The first thing he and Kelly did was unzip them and slip off the big doughnut headsets so they hung around their necks.

Ben unzipped a pocket in his trousers, took out a bottle of sun cream and smeared some on his face and arms. It felt gritty where the red dust had stuck to his skin.

Kelly couldn't resist a mocking remark. 'Gotta protect that lily-white English complexion, eh, Ben? Your mom's got you well trained.'

Ben snapped the lid shut and held the bottle out. 'Don't you want some? George isn't going to fancy you if you come back looking like a lobster.'

Kelly hooked a bottle of water out from behind her seat and drained it. She looked at the empty container with disappointment. 'I don't suppose you've got any spare water?' she said hopefully.

Ben pointed to a sign at the end of the avenue of trees. It said: FORREST VALE VISITOR CENTRE, ONE KILO-METRE, with an arrow pointing to a path to the right. 'I haven't, but they're bound to have some at the visitor centre. Will the plane be all right if we leave it?'

Kelly leaned into the cockpit, checked the

brake, then closed the door. 'Yeah, it should be fine.'

As they set off, the leaves of the vines started to rustle around them like a whispering crowd. The branches, tied in orderly rows, waved and rippled.

Kelly stopped and slipped her orange baseball cap off. Her blonde hair billowed out behind her and she tilted her head back. 'Mmm, that is nice.'

Then the wind changed direction. Suddenly it was a lot stronger. The vines flapped the other way, straining against their tethers. Big leaves plunged down on Kelly's face like fingers trying to gather her up. She jumped backwards. The wind pushed her back even further and she staggered into Ben. Ben would have fallen over, but the wind changed again and for a moment they were stuck together, unable to move forwards. The wind had to be over sixty miles an hour – it was impossible to take even a step. Then, as quickly as it had sprung up, the wind dropped to a dead calm.

Kelly bundled her hair up and put her hat back on. 'Man, this weather is freaky today. It's a good thing we're down here and not trying to fly in it.'

* * *

Matt and Jenny Forrest, and their army of helpers, stood around the picnic tables. All the guests had arrived and Matt was pouring glasses of last year's vintage while Jenny handed them out.

Suddenly the checked rug on the table billowed up like a sail. Matt tried to grab the wine glasses but they crashed over, sending Chardonnay and broken glass all over his bare legs. The chairs set out in a row next to the decking folded up by themselves and keeled over. Sun hats were snatched off the visitors' heads and whirled into the air.

There was a sound of screeching, like fingernails down a blackboard. Moments later a tangle of metal landed on the parched earth. The wind had torn the TV aerial off the roof.

'Inside!' Jenny yelled. Her voice was a tiny thing against the wind roaring in her ears. She waved her arms towards the house.

Her guests, half blinded by dust blowing in off the vineyards, struggled after her.

Once they were all inside, Matt pulled the door shut with difficulty. They looked out at the hillside. The vines were shaking violently. Dark clouds were drifting across the sapphire-blue sky.

Jenny's father shook dust out of his grey hair. 'Of all days to get rain . . .'

'Maybe it isn't rain,' said Matt. 'It wasn't earlier.'

'Dust or rain . . .' Jenny sighed. 'Someone up there must have it in for us . . .'

The clouds massed up from behind the hill, hugging the ground. There was another vineyard there, belonging to the Forrests' neighbour.

'I've never seen rain looking like that,' said Jenny's father.

In the distance, the cloud began to creep over the hill. The landscape looked like someone had smudged its edges with charcoal.

Jenny grabbed the binoculars they kept on the windowsill. As she turned the focus wheel she saw flickering tongues of orange flame.

It wasn't rain approaching . . .

The binoculars fell from her hand as she gasped: 'Fire!'

Alex Porter and his wife Jacquetta were on holiday, over from New Zealand. They'd hired a Toyota

Corolla in Adelaide and had headed out into the hills to tour the wine-growing region.

The air conditioning was on full blast in the car, but it was barely coping with the heat. Jacquetta fanned herself with the map on her knee. Outside, the rows of vines looked like they were wilting. The grapes hung in tight clusters, a blue bloom on the skins, ready for picking.

'Those grapes must be tough,' she said. 'I can't understand why they're not shrivelled to raisins by now.'

Suddenly Alex found he couldn't see the dials on the dashboard. The sky outside had gone dark. He flicked the lights on. 'Hey, looks like we're in for a storm.'

'We certainly could use it.' Jacquetta turned the dial on the air conditioning but it was already at maximum. 'Look at the temperature,' she said, pointing to the dashboard display. 'It's fifty degrees outside. I thought it was supposed to get colder before a storm, not hotter.'

'Fifty degrees?' Alex tapped the display. 'That can't be right. There must be something wrong with it.' He swung the car round the corner.

Then they saw why it was getting so hot and so

dark. In front of them, the vineyard was a wall of flame the height of a two-storey building. It rolled towards them, roaring and crackling.

Jacquetta screamed.

Alex slammed on the brakes, jammed the car into reverse, screeched through a turn, then when they were facing back the way they came, he gunned the accelerator.

Jacquetta twisted in her seat, staring back through the rear windscreen. The fire was an orange ball, boiling towards them.

'Faster, Alex! It's going to catch us!'

Alex kept his foot flat on the floor. They reached 80 kph, then 90. A bend came up. He was going too fast. The back end of the car swung like an opening gate and crunched into some vines. The impact knocked Jacquetta's head hard against the window. She slumped down, unconscious.

They had come to a standstill. Alex revved the engine. The wheels spun on the dusty track. In his rear-view mirror he caught a glimpse of the flames drawing nearer. Smoke started to seep into the car.

Then the tyres bit and the Toyota moved off again.

But the fire was gaining. Flames began to light up the darkened interior of the car, flickering over Jacquetta's face. She was moving her head groggily and muttering. There was blood coming out of one of her ears. That shocked him for a moment and he stopped concentrating on driving.

His hesitation cost them vital seconds. The flames in the rear-view mirror were now much closer. Alex pushed the pedal to the floor. Another corner was coming up. He threw the steering wheel to the side –

– and saw the headlights of the pick-up truck coming towards him. He didn't have time to stop or swerve. There was nowhere to go anyway. Alex glimpsed the horrified face of the driver in the cab, then the two vehicles crunched together. Jacquetta and Alex were thrown against the windscreen.

Their seat belts stopped them going all the way through, but the impact knocked them out cold. The truck driver looked up and saw the wall of flames boiling over the car towards him.

As the heat ignited their petrol tank, Alex and Jacquetta were mercifully no longer aware.

Chapter Nine

Kelly only just managed to grab her hat in time. The wind was gusting one way and then another like it was playing with them.

'You see,' she said, 'you can't possibly fly a microlight in these conditions.'

Even a half-wit would know that, thought Ben. She was obviously thinking, *He's thirteen, he must be a moron*. Well, he knew how to deal with that. Putting on an innocent face, he said: 'What if we can't take off again?'

'Of course we can take off,' said Kelly. 'We have to wait till the weather changes, though.'

'I know that,' said Ben, still acting innocent. 'But George's shift ends at three. And we've still got to get back.'

'If I miss him today there's always tomorrow. Then I'll be footloose and fancy free.'

Ben played his trump card. 'George is going on holiday tomorrow.'

Kelly looked at him sceptically.

'It said so in his records,' said Ben.

He couldn't help laughing. But as he did so, he got a lungful of smoke that kicked off a coughing fit. All of a sudden his eyes were watering. Through the tears he saw thick black smoke and smelled burning. Where was that coming from? Had somebody lit a bonfire in the middle of the vineyard?

Kelly grabbed him and shrieked, 'Fire!'

A mass of tumbling, burning branches blasted towards them.

They turned and hared back the way they'd come. It was uphill, and strenuous going in the strong mid-afternoon heat. Ben could feel the smoke in his throat. It was hard to get his breath but adrenaline gave him a burst of speed.

Kelly looked back. From the vantage point of the brow of the hill, she saw a wall of flame stretching right across the vineyard. The wind was fanning it towards them.

'The whole place is on fire!' she yelled. 'We can't outrun it!'

They turned the corner by the signpost and saw the microlight a little further up, that funny glass-pod body with a white fabric wing on top and a tricycle underneath. It looked flimsy, but with flames raging at gale-speed through the tinder-dry vegetation, their only chance was to get airborne.

A flaming branch whirled past Ben's ear. It landed in the vines. He heard the crackle as the dry leaves started to smoulder.

He reached the plane before Kelly and tried to undo the catch on the door one-handed, his other arm up, shielding his face from more burning debris.

Kelly got her door open, but then another gust of wind brought hot stinging sparks.

She screamed and climbed up onto the wing.

Ben hoisted himself up on the other side to see what

was wrong and saw that the wing was covered in debris, glowing like hot coals.

Kelly grabbed a blackened branch as big as a butcher's bone and hurled it away. 'Get them off! They'll burn a hole and then the plane's useless!'

Ben pulled his sleeve down over his arm and swept it over the wing. The embers left sooty marks on the stiff white material, but luckily there were no burn holes. Kelly cleared the other side.

They got down and scrambled into the plane.

The engine spluttered into life. To their right, the vines were starting to burn. Ben could feel the heat through the back of the cockpit. Kelly increased the revs and took the plane jolting up the path. Her headset was still around her neck – there wasn't a second to waste. Ben was sorry he'd made jokes about not being able to take off in that wind. Would they manage it now?

They started to lift off the ground, but the wind blew them sideways and Ben felt the vines swish along the undercarriage like a row of hands trying to grab the wheels. Kelly had the throttle all the way forwards but the microlight was still trying to go sideways. Then suddenly it soared upwards and they were leaving the vegetation behind.

Ben breathed a silent prayer of relief.

They climbed up into the sky. Clouds of smoke turned the windscreen black, filling their mouths with a gritty, pungent taste. Glowing embers like red fire-flies whirled past them. Then the black clouds were behind them and they were flying into sunlight again.

Down below, smoke was billowing up out of the vineyard.

The plane suddenly dropped like a stone.

'A thermal!' Kelly screamed. 'You have control! More throttle! More throttle now!'

Ben felt beside him. His fingers grasped the handle and he pulled it upwards. The engine grew louder. He didn't even have time to question why she wanted him to take control now, of all times.

'Grab the stick! Get the nose up!' called Kelly.

Ben pulled the stick back. He felt the pedals moving beside his feet as Kelly operated them. The microlight stopped plummeting and started to climb. There was another moment of dark smoke clouds, then bright sunshine.

Ben suddenly realized there was rather a lot of blue sky on his side of the plane, while through Kelly's window there was a dramatic view of the ground.

Kelly whacked the stick with her left forearm. The view out of the windows evened out, with a proper amount of sky on each side.

'Level out! Let the stick go!' She was still shouting – she hadn't yet put her headset on. It was still around her neck. Then Ben noticed she was holding her hands oddly, like she was trying to avoid touching the palms to anything.

And why was she making him do the flying at such a crucial stage?

He reached across and placed her headset over her ears so that he could talk to her.

'Kelly, why am I in control?'

Kelly looked down at the palms of her hands. Ben reached over to see what was wrong but she flinched and pulled them away before he'd even touched her.

'You've burned your hands.'

Kelly nodded. 'You're going to have to go from basic training to graduation in one lesson. I'll tell you what to do – but you've got to fly this thing home.'

* * *

The hills around Adelaide were covered in vineyards. Nobody knew which one started burning first, and how exactly the fire had begun. But once it took hold it roared easily through the endless lines of parched, dry plants in a matter of minutes. Even where the leaves were not in direct contact with flames, the surrounding heat scorched them. This made the vegetation give off gases, which, because of the heat, started to burn spontaneously. The blazing hills created their own weather system, sucking in air to feed the flames, like a fire drawing air from a chimney. The fire gobbled up acre after acre until it reached the red, dusty outback.

And as well as travelling outwards, the fire also swept inwards. The first places it reached were Adelaide's many parks and green spaces on the out-skirts of the town.

Victoria Shilton stood in the circle of emerald-green grass. Her eyes were on only one thing: the little dimpled ball in front of her feet, just metres away from the seventeenth hole. On the fairways, the grass of the golf course was parched to the colour of straw, but around the holes it had been watered to keep the surface perfect.

A gust of wind tugged at Victoria's hat, sending the brim flopping down over one eye. The wind had been getting more and more erratic since they'd set off from the clubhouse after lunch, but they were nearly at the end of the course and Victoria was determined to finish. She had noticed a scent of smoke and heard the distant wail of sirens, but she was a dedicated sportswoman and had learned to let nothing distract her. She pushed the hat back off her brow to concentrate better, and the wind snatched it right off her head.

She didn't see where it went; she would get it in a minute. Right now, she was in the zone, a state of perfect concentration. Just a gentle tap and the ball should roll into the hole. Victoria breathed in, ready to play the stroke.

A voice suddenly ruined her concentration. 'Strewth!' It was her opponent, a Thai restaurateur who she knew only by the name Troy. Victoria whirled round, ready to give him some choice words for spoiling her shot.

Troy was pointing at the rough – the woodland

around the seventeenth hole. Flames were crackling through the trees, sending smoke rolling towards them.

Victoria was so startled she dropped her club. 'Oh my God.'

They stood, stunned, as they watched the orange flames licking through the wood, catching anything they touched and sending it luminous with flame. In no more than thirty seconds the entire wood was on fire, all the way back down the edge of the fairway. The wind was whipping it up into an inferno.

Troy slid his iron back into his trolley. 'We'd better get the groundsman.' He turned and set off down the green.

Victoria grabbed her trolley and hurried after him.

Then something very strange happened. The wind snatched up some burning branches, carried them over Victoria's head and dashed them against the trees on the other side of the fairway, several metres away.

Like a spark jumping a gap, the fire was leaping through the crowns of the trees.

On both sides of them, the woods were on fire.

Victoria and Troy forgot about their trolleys. They ran for their lives.

* * *

The golf course backed onto the racecourse. So far, two races had been run since the wind started to pick up, but things were getting worse.

The wind was upsetting the horses, filling their sensitive ears with strange noises. They could hear everything that was going on in the adjoining streets – dustbins falling over, gates banging and trees creaking. To these highly strung creatures it sounded like a riot was coming their way.

Another race was due to start but the jockeys couldn't get their mounts into the starting gates. The wind was making them rattle. To the horses it sounded like the metal bars would collapse on top of them. It was too much for their taut nerves.

When the jockeys tried to whip the horses in, they wheeled round and reared. The jockeys pulled them up, turned them back and urged them towards the gates again. The horses rebelled and tried to gallop away. Now they were all spinning in circles, dust kicking up from their hooves, looking at the gates with terrified eyes.

The stand was next to the starting gates, filled, even

on a weekday, with a couple of hundred people. Most of them were racing professionals – trainers, owners, potential buyers, newspaper reporters and bookies. All of them watched anxiously as the young thoroughbreds spun round and round. Those graceful legs were so easily injured – and that might write off an expensive horse. But these seasoned racegoers had seen plenty of equine tantrums before. If the horses got into the starting gates they could run the adrenaline out of their systems safely.

All eyes in the spectators' stand were on the horses. No one noticed the deadly cinders that were blowing in from the golf course next door.

At first a few flaming leaves flew over. They landed on the roof of the stand and on the piles of rubbish that had fallen out of the bins. The greasy papers from the nearby burger stall caught in seconds.

The smoke reached the sensitive nostrils of the horses below, but they were already so upset that it made little difference.

Some burning twigs blew as far as the car park. Many of the grooms had tied haynets to the horse-boxes for the horses to eat while they were being rubbed down. The hay was dry and glowing embers set it alight in no time. The burning debris blew in easily through the open ramps. The horseboxes, already hot as ovens from the sun, were soon ablaze.

In the spectator stand, the organizers were discussing whether the wind meant they should cancel the rest of the day's racing. At first no one spotted the fires taking hold all around them.

Out on the track, a big black yearling had had enough. It leaped into the air with a twisting buck. The jockey didn't have a chance of staying in the saddle. He pitched straight over the horse's shoulder. The loose horse now took off in a flat-out gallop away from the rattling gates. It crashed through the white rails as though they were matchwood.

On the other side was a row of cars parked tightly together. The horse saw there was no gap, so it tried to jump a green Ford.

It misjudged and landed on the car. The impact made a sickening noise. The horse crashed to the ground, twisted up onto its feet like a cat and carried on fleeing, sparks flying off its shoes.

The car was a write-off. Its bonnet was crushed, its

roof staved in. Being hit by half a ton of horse travelling at 65 kph had the same result as a head-on collision with another car.

While everyone's eyes were on the galloping horse, the roof of the stand had reached flashpoint. Inside, a reporter from the *Adelaide Herald* heard part of the roof collapse behind him. He turned round and saw that the back of the stand had disappeared behind a pall of thick black smoke. Little tongues of orange flame were flickering all around him.

'Fire!' he screamed. 'Get out! Get out!'

The spectators could only run in one direction – under the white rails and onto the racecourse.

Meanwhile the loose horse was heading towards the car park. Just then, one of the horseboxes exploded as the fire reached its fuel tank.

The loose horse immediately whirled round and fled back towards the other horses, which were still milling around by the starting gates. When they saw the terror in its eyes, they panicked, and the jockeys lost all control of their mounts.

There was only one way for the petrified horses to go: through the rattling gates.

But because the race hadn't yet started, the exit doors were bolted. The galloping horses crashed into the gates, pulling them right off their foundations.

The spectators who had fled from the burning stands reached the grass and paused for breath. Behind them, the stand was a mass of flame.

Too late they felt the ground shaking, as it does at the start of a race. Ten horses, imprisoned in the closed gates, were charging towards them.

Chapter Ten

It was bad being on the ground, but it was just as bad being off it. The air was seething with thermals.

So far, Ben's first experience of flying had been the kind that would put most people off for life. Since they'd taken off from the vineyard it had been like riding a rollercoaster – an extreme rollercoaster that didn't even stop to let you get your breath.

Kelly didn't stop for breath either. She yelled instructions relentlessly:

'More throttle!'

'Stick right!'

'Stick up!'

'Stick up now, Ben, *now!*'

He didn't think, he just did what he was told. It was like they were one creature. She was the brains and he was the body.

A body that was feeling exceedingly sick.

The microlight dropped 20 feet. Ben was lifted out of his seat: the seat belt cut into his legs and his head bashed against the window frame.

Kelly screamed and the sound drilled into his ear drums. She must have banged her hands – she kept doing that. Judging by the level of discomfort, she probably had some second-degree burns. Those would need medical attention soon.

As suddenly as the plane had dropped, Ben found that they were flying smoothly along again.

He glanced at Kelly. The map was on her knee. She was leaning over it, holding it down with her elbows. Her hands were clasped out of the way so they wouldn't touch anything inadvertently. She was also very quiet.

Ben kept expecting the plane to start plummeting again but for now they seemed to have escaped the turbulence. He peered out of the window. Below was an unbroken mass of smoke. He couldn't tell if they were over vineyards or suburbs – or even the outback. There were isolated patches where the wind had cleared the smoke and he could see bright fires burning below. He got his mobile out of his flying suit. 'Is it safe to use this here? My mum's down there somewhere and I want to see if she's all right.'

Kelly nodded towards a slot on the dashboard, like a hands-free set in a car. 'Put it in there.'

Ben set up the phone, then pressed a speed dial.

A recorded voice came through on their headsets: '*Lines are busy. Please try again later.*'

'Could you try my dad?' Kelly was pointing at the zip pocket on her trousers. 'My cell phone's in here. Increase height by about fifty feet before you do.'

Ben opened the throttle a little, then fished her phone out and slotted it into the dashboard cradle.

'He's on speed dial, under "Dad".'

Ben pressed the navigation key. The picture of Kelly dangling from the power chute glowed briefly, then was replaced by her speed dial menu. He cursored down and dialled.

The response was the same: '*Lines are busy* . . .' Ben cut the call.

Kelly checked over the instruments. 'Bit more left rudder,' she said.

Ben obliged – though he could see that her mind was elsewhere.

She voiced what they were both thinking. 'Your mom and my dad were in the same place, so I suppose it makes sense that neither of them was contactable. We'll try again in a while, huh?' She winced as she talked.

'We'd better get you to a doctor,' said Ben.

Kelly looked down at the map. She had been leaning on it while the plane was throwing them around and now it was creased like a well-used cushion. She tried to smooth it down, having to use her elbows. 'For sure. I just need to find somewhere we can land.'

Rikki stood at the window. She always liked to watch the racehorses from her tenth-storey apartment. That was why the block had appealed to her and her husband so much. Now the afternoon's racing was part of her daily routine with her three-month-old son Josh. As usual, she fed him, changed him and walked around the living room with him on her hip, jogging him to sleep while she watched the 1.45 yearlings race.

But today she looked out of the window and got the shock of her life.

The stand was engulfed in a ball of flame. Black smoke boiled into the sky. The horses had started running before the gates had opened. They had dragged the entire structure out of the ground and were galloping caged inside it.

Right in their path were the people who had fled from the flames. They had no chance of getting away. The charging horses knocked them down like a monstrous war machine.

She couldn't look any more and turned away. The baby picked up on her shock and started to cry.

Rikki had friends on the other side of the race-course: Molly and Dan. Molly had a daughter the same age as Josh and usually tried to get her off to sleep by the 1.45 race. Could she see this too? Rikki sat down on the sofa, being careful to support Josh's head properly, picked up the phone and pressed a speed dial.

While it was ringing, she glanced out of the window and got another shock. She couldn't see the carnage on the racetrack any longer. Smoke obscured it all. The entire horizon seemed to be carpeted in black smoke and flickering orange flames. Blue lights flashed beneath the smoke as though travelling under black gauze.

As she waited for Molly to pick up the phone, another thought crossed her mind. Would the fire reach the flat? Surely not; it was ten storeys up.

But why hadn't Molly answered yet?

Suddenly the line went dead.

The phone rang for a short time in Molly's house, but she wasn't able to reach it. She was trying desperately to open the window onto the balcony. Her baby, Emanuelle, was in a neoprene sling on her chest.

The security locks wouldn't budge. Behind her, the sofa was on fire. The tapestry cushions and upholstery were nearly all consumed, and the bare frame was showing through the orange flames like a

Terminator's skeleton. Thick smoke poured from the foam interior. Outside the room the hall was a wreckage of burning rafters.

Molly had the key in the window lock, but it was stiff and she couldn't turn it. Emanuelle was crying and coughing, her face scrunched and red. Hot smoke burned the inside of her lungs. It felt like she had sucked in boiling water. It must be even worse for her baby.

The key slipped out of Molly's fingers. She gave a strangled sob of despair and fell to her knees. Once she was down on the floor, the smoke got even thicker. She coughed, but there was no oxygen, only the choking black smoke and the fumes from the sofa. She could hardly even see Emanuelle's face barely inches away. She collapsed while the phone rang and rang.

The flames reached the phone cables, shrivelling them like burning hair. The ringing stopped and the LCD display in the phone station blistered in the heat.

By then the fire had spread to the building next door to Molly's . . .

* * *

The pall of smoke drifted across the city. The botanical gardens, which Engine 33 had fought so hard to save, went up like a bonfire. Wanasri and her crew couldn't save it now; they were tied up with other fires. Every fire engine in the city was out on a call, fighting flash blazes. They worked fast, but the fires travelled faster.

Once the fire had taken hold in the outskirts, it began to move towards the city centre.

In the main precinct the staff of the law courts were in the middle of an ordinary working day when they were alerted by the fire alarm. They filed down the stairs, some of them escorting bewildered clients. They assumed it was a false alarm or a fire drill – until they reached the street and saw the mushroom cloud of smoke against the sky.

The dentist's practice next door was on fire. Firefighters were pumping water in through the upstairs windows; smoke and steam were pouring out. More firefighters ushered the solicitors away to the end of the street, where paramedics were holding a breathing mask over the face of a young woman. She had blood dripping out of her mouth and had obviously been in the middle of an extraction when the alarm sounded. The dentist and his nurse were trying to comfort her, their white coats spattered with her blood.

A woman in a fluorescent coat was evacuating another building. The people pouring out were bare-foot and wore loose, pyjama-like clothes. Some of them carried brightly coloured mats under their arms. They had been in the middle of a relaxing yoga class and looked as dazed as the dental patient to find themselves outside.

Not all the evacuations were so peaceful. In a pedestrianized street just a hundred metres away, the usual lunchtime crowds were enjoying a snack at the many cafés and bars, protected from the sun by fringed umbrellas. One minute they were discussing whether to go indoors because it had got windy. The next, they were enveloped in burning fabric as the umbrellas caught light.

The high buildings turned the precinct into a wind tunnel. As punters knocked over tables in their panic, a gale ripped through the burning awnings. Those who were still able to run were pursued down the streets by pieces of flaming fabric.

The promenade on the west side of town was a mass of people fleeing from the marinas, restaurants and hotels. They ran out onto the jetties, crowded into boats and pushed off into the bay. A pair of old women, their skin leathery from too much sun, were struggling with their boat. As one of them started the engine and the other tried to untie the mooring rope, three waiters wearing name badges from the nearby St Michael's restaurant ran up and made for the rail. The woman at the helm screamed in fury and pointed a flare pistol at them, forcing the waiters to retreat to the quay. The second woman finally freed the boat and they set off, still keeping an eye on the waiters to make sure they didn't try to climb aboard.

Soon the bay was bustling with flapping sails. The passengers in the boats looked back at the city in astonishment. Wherever they looked, from the hotels at the water's edge to the hills away in the distance, were smoke and flames.

Chapter Eleven

At the conference centre, the public debate was scheduled to start in a few minutes.

The Oz Protectors were at the front of the queue. Timi, Amy and Joseph were first in through the doors, carrying their banner with the message: STOP SECRET US EXPERIMENTS. Timi had gone through a lot to be there. He was skipping classes at college and now he had lost his car. He felt pent-up and angry, looking to make somebody pay.

The two other members of the Adelaide branch were also cutting classes. Wez and his girlfriend Bo had been giving out leaflets in the centre of town since early that morning. They believed in their cause, and had ensured that a good crowd turned up. Soon that American major, colonel or whatever he was, would be answering some hard questions on live TV. The Australian public would be horrified when they learned what had been going on out in the desert.

Banners had to be left in the foyer. 'Just toss it any-where, chum,' said a security guard. 'Nobody's going to pinch the bloomin' thing, are they?'

Timi propped the banner next to one showing an Uncle Sam skull, then guided his companions through a side passageway. He had done casual jobs as a bouncer when rock concerts were held at the conference centre and knew the short cuts to the best seats.

They claimed a front row position and sat down.

Amy looked around the auditorium. 'I don't see any TV cameras.'

'They'll be round the back setting up,' said Timi. 'That's what they do when they record concerts. They park the outside broadcast lorry in the alley at the back and the cameras transmit to it—'

The rest of his words were cut off by the fire alarm.

Timi couldn't believe it. 'Of all the times to hold a fire drill . . .'

Amy looked around to see what everyone else was doing. 'Do we have to go out? Maybe we can just stay here.'

Conference centre officials appeared at the doors, wearing fluorescent vests and armbands. They beckoned people towards the fire exits.

A voice came over the tannoy: '*Ladies and gentlemen, we respectfully request that you vacate the building. The public debate will take place at another time.*'

Timi felt like spitting with rage. Amy and Wez pushed him along towards the door.

'I haven't been breaking my ass all morning for the debate to be cancelled!' Timi's English was slipping again as he became angry. He lapsed into a torrent of angry-sounding Korean.

'It's a conspiracy, mate, is what it is,' reckoned Wez. 'They don't want us to be heard. The Pentagon will have made some calls and they've got these blokes here jumping through hoops.'

They reached the corridor, but as the crowd turned

right, Timi, Amy and Wez hung back to wait for Bo and Joseph.

Bo touched Timi's arm and pointed behind them.

Coming down the corridor from the other direction was a petite woman wearing a slightly crumpled safari suit, with a determined expression and straight red hair. She was talking to the American army guy.

Wez bristled. 'There he is, about to get away scot-free.'

'No he isn't,' said Timi. He strode up to Bel and Major Kurtis. The others followed.

'Dr Kelland? Major? I know a quicker way out. Go back the way you came.'

The major hesitated, but Bel turned round immediately and quickly set off down the corridor. The major could barely keep up with her.

Following behind Timi, Amy bit her lip. What was he up to? she wondered.

Timi directed Bel and the major into the maze of passages behind the stage. After a few turnings he pulled open a door. 'Stop, stop,' he called. 'You've overshot – it's this way.'

Bel followed his instructions: like most forthright people, her first assumption was always that others were telling her the truth. Major Kurtis and the Oz Protectors hurried along behind her.

But then Bel realized where they were and looked round. 'I think we must have taken a wrong turn. This is the janitor's office.'

Timi stood in the doorway, blocking her exit. 'No we haven't taken a wrong turn, Dr Kelland.' He nodded at the others. 'We need to get the major.' Then he grabbed Major Kurtis and pinned his arms behind his back. Although uncertain, Wez stepped forward to help; he was as tall as the older man and could subdue him easily.

The colour drained from Bel's face. 'What is this?'

Timi ignored her. 'Major,' he said in a dangerously calm voice, 'I must ask you to come with us.'

Bel's words came out as a rasp: 'What do you want?'

The fire alarm was still ringing. 'Let's get out,' said Joseph. 'Shall we take her as well?'

Bel spoke through white lips. 'Are you kidnapping us?'

'We don't need to take her,' said Bo. 'Shall we let her go?'

Wez shook his head. 'She'll raise the alarm.' His eyes were wide behind his glasses. Caught up in the sudden turn of events, following Timi's lead, he had a fanatical look.

Timi decided: 'We'll bring the major out here. Lock her in.'

Wez frogmarched the major back into the corridor, then Bo shut the door on Bel, dragged a chair across and jammed it up against the door, under the handle. The door thundered as Bel's fists pounded on it. The handle jerked up and down, but with the chair under it she couldn't turn it. And with the noise of the fire alarm no one would hear her.

'We can't leave her here . . .' said Amy uncertainly, looking back at the door as she followed the others out.

'Once the fire drill's over somebody will soon find her,' said Bo. 'Come on, Ames.'

The corridor led to the back entrance, where the TV crew would be parked. Timi grabbed the major's pinioned arm and jerked it forwards. 'Walk. You're going to tell the nation about those experiments you've been doing.'

The major did as he was told, but said nothing.

Amy ran ahead. 'I'll go and tell the TV guys we're coming.'

Bo joined her and the two girls sprinted down the corridor. They pushed open the double doors at the end and went out onto the metal gantry of the fire escape.

A moment later they came back.

'There's no news crew here,' called Bo.

Timi grabbed the major's arm and pushed him the rest of the way up the corridor and out of the door. He stood on the metal gantry by the goods entrance, looking around in disbelief. The alleyway was full of smoke, and there was no sign of a TV crew.

'Oh my God.' Joseph pointed upwards and the others followed his terrified gaze.

The entire sky had changed colour. It was filled with boiling clouds of black and orange. Sirens wailed and, at the end of the alleyway, a fire engine roared past, its blue lights cutting through the smog like bolts of lightning.

Amy realized that people were running past in the street. 'We'd better get out of here,' she said.

'No,' snarled Timi. 'We're going to do the interview ourselves. Bo, get out your phone.'

'Don't be an idiot, Tim,' said Amy. 'We should go.'

Bo was looking at the display on her phone, lining up the shot. 'Ready. Timi, you get in there next to the major.'

Timi looked the major full in the eye. 'Your listening station in Coober Pedy. What's really going on there?'

Major Kurtis kept his face impassive. He spoke patiently and calmly. 'I don't know what you're talking about.'

Wez tightened his grip on the major's other arm. 'You're lying.'

Timi kicked the major in the shin. He winced at the pain.

'So why is the population out there getting so ill? What are you messing with? Is it biological warfare? Radioactive fallout?'

The major let out a long, slow breath, composing himself. He looked away from Timi, directly into the camera. 'This is a free country. If you have a reasonable objection you can make it democratically. You don't have to do it with violence.'

Timi had had enough. 'You lying bastard.' He pulled something out of his pocket. A long blade glinted in his hand. A flick knife.

Amy, Wez, Joseph and Bo gasped in horror. The major stiffened with shock. Wez momentarily loosened his grip on the major's arms, but the man was surrounded so he wasn't going anywhere.

Timi grabbed the major's lapel and pressed the blade against the skin of his throat. 'You think you can keep a thing like this covered up, you arrogant bastard? I'll tell you what I'm going to do; I'm going to make you talk.'

Bo looked at Amy. Her eyes were fearful and brimming with tears. Amy reached her hand towards Timi's arm, but didn't dare touch him. Wez tightened his grip on the major again. Joseph looked as though he wanted to run away.

The major swallowed. His Adam's apple went up and down his throat, making the gleaming blade rise and fall. 'I will offer no resistance,' he said. The words sounded like a standard phrase learned on some military course.

'You're damn right,' snarled Timi. 'Now, tell the camera – what's going on in Coober Pedy?'

The major looked at his captor. A bead of sweat trickled down his forehead. 'I'm afraid I can't answer that.'

Bo gave a sob and buried her face in Amy's shoulder. Amy put an arm around her and looked at the major, pleading: 'Just tell him, for pity's sake!'

The janitor's room was small and windowless – it was really just a large cupboard. The only light came from a row of glass bricks in the top of the wall and there was no ventilation.

Bel rattled the door handle, but there was something against the door stopping the handle from turning all the way.

Then she realized that she could smell smoke – it was drifting in under the door.

So it wasn't a fire drill. Bel felt herself starting to panic, but her iron will took control just in time. After a minute of shouting at the top of her voice she slumped against the door, exhausted.

The fire alarm continued to ring and she could hear sirens. A lot of sirens.

Were all those fire engines for this one building? What on earth had happened?

A sturdy broom was propped up inside the door. She pulled the head off it so that she was left with a long wooden pole. She slipped the pole under the door and wiggled it around. She felt it hit something but she couldn't tell what it was. Bashing it a couple of times failed to dislodge it.

Pulling the broom handle back in, she looked around the room for inspiration. Was there anything else she could use? The room contained a table with a kettle, some mugs and a portable CD player.

Bel picked up the CD player and snapped it open. Inside was a disc. She hurried back to the door and slipped her hand underneath, angling the shiny side of the disc. The image wasn't as clear as a mirror but it was just enough to show her why the door wouldn't open. The Oz Protectors had wedged a chair under the handle.

Bel felt a flash of anger. They'd locked her in and left her to burn. When she got out somebody was going to pay.

She pulled the CD back in, pushed the pole out against one of the chair legs and levered the chair out of the way. There was a clattering noise, then she found she could turn the handle and the door opened.

The corridor was hazy with smoke.

'Hello?' called Bel. Smoke caught her throat and she started coughing. She couldn't hear anything over the screaming alarm.

She had to get out, but which way? This backstage part of the building was a warren of narrow corridors and staircases and she didn't know the layout.

The smoke was blowing in from the right. To the left was a glowing FIRE EXIT sign over a door. Bel hurried over to it and seized the handle. It was hot but she pulled it open anyway.

The other side was a thick veil of smoke and a red glow, like burning coals. Air rushed in from the open door and in moments bright orange flames were leaping out at her.

Bel turned and raced back down the corridor, nearly

falling over in her strappy sandals. 'Doc Martens next time,' she told herself.

Flames roared out of the room and pursued her, travelling fast as they took hold of the polystyrene ceiling tiles.

Seeing another door ahead of her, she peered through the glass and spotted a staircase leading up. Should she go upwards? Wouldn't it be better to find a way out on the ground floor?

Then she noticed fumes curling in wisps from the ceiling tiles further along. She wasn't a materials scientist, but she guessed the fumes were toxic. And they seemed heavier than air. Going up was probably the only option if she wanted to avoid being poisoned.

She took the stairs two at a time and came out in another corridor. She ran down to the end and emerged on the upstairs gallery, where big windows looked out onto a paved area and shops beyond.

For a moment she thought she was seeing things. The street outside was shrouded in a thick fog of smoke. Shapes moved around in it. Some were people, some were emergency vehicles. She could see pockets of orange flame and flashes of blue light. Several other buildings in the street seemed to be on fire. It looked more like *War of the Worlds* than the Adelaide business district.

She ran over to a window and hammered on the glass. Surely someone would look up from the street and see her. No one did. She examined the window frames, but they were solid and could not be opened. Bel whirled round, looking desperately for another way out, and saw a fire exit sign by the refreshment bar. She ran across and seized the handle. It burned her palm.

She backed away. She knew now what that meant: fire on the other side of the door.

There must be another fire exit, she thought. Then she saw the sign for the ladies' toilet. That was bound to have an outside window for ventilation. The handle wasn't hot so she pushed through the two sets of swing doors—

Only to find that there were no windows. Just an electric extractor fan.

She came back out again and saw another fire exit sign pointing to the stock room behind the refreshment bar. As she made her way through, the first thing that hit her was a smell of roasting. Along one wall boxes of crisps smouldered: they had set fire to the curtain at the end, but beyond that was a long window with a door leading out to a balcony.

Bel was about to make a dash for it when she realized that the carpet tiles were smoking. Her shoes were too flimsy to protect her if she ran across.

She grabbed a blue fire extinguisher off the wall and showered the carpet tiles with white powder. But the fat in the crisps had melted the plastic wrappers and soaked into the cardboard and the carpet tiles and was keeping them burning. She emptied the entire extinguisher over the floor but the heat was still too intense. The carpet tiles were starting to bubble as the rubber underneath melted. Bel threw down the extinguisher in despair.

Then she realized that she could still reach the other end of the window. Maybe there was another opening there.

But she found only a big expanse of glass. The only exit door was behind the burning curtain.

Bel ran back and retrieved the extinguisher. Even empty, it was as heavy as a dumb-bell. She held it like a baseball bat and whacked the glass nearest to her with all her strength. The window turned frosty and shattered, and she stumbled out, her feet skidding on nuggets of glass.

She ran along the balcony and down a fire escape to the street. She was out.

But maybe not safe yet. The street was full of smoke and teeming with firefighters and emergency vehicles. All the buildings she could see were on fire. Flames ringed the whole area, sending a tunnel of smoke up into the sky.

As she emerged, a firefighter approached her – a young woman with oriental features and smudged stripes on her face. She looked astonished to see Bel. 'Where did you come from?'

Bel indicated the broken window. 'In case of emergency, break the glass.' She looked around. The only people she could see were firefighters. She felt disorientated and alone. 'Where are all the delegates from the conference?'

Wanasri pointed down the road. 'They were evacuated to the green.'

'Maybe not all of them,' said Bel. 'I was with an

American army officer and some protestors. We were right at the back of the building.'

'Then they could still be trapped inside.' Wanasri turned to a burly firefighter beside her. 'Darren, we'd better get a crew into this building before the roof caves in.'

Chapter Twelve

Kelly looked over the instruments. She checked the height, the windspeed and their bearing, then sat back. 'We're going steadily and conditions seem to be good. I could use some first aid. You can let go of the controls.'

Cautiously, Ben let go of the stick and the throttle. 'How long can I leave them for?'

'Well, you wouldn't have time for an appendectomy, but you can bandage my hands. Do it quickly though.'

'Where's the first-aid kit?' said Ben.

'It's your water bottle and my scarf,' said Kelly.

'Hmm. Well, next time you might want to pack some plasters.' Ben reached for the gold and black scarf around Kelly's neck. He unfastened it, tore it into two long strips and poured water from his bottle over them.

Kelly managed a chuckle. 'That scarf belongs to my mom. It's Versace. If she saw you doing that she'd skin you alive.' Very gingerly, she held her left hand out for Ben to bandage.

Ben was shocked at the sight of her burns. The skin was charred and weeping. He started the bandage around her fingers so that he could secure it tightly, then took it across the burned flesh. Kelly went still as a statue, trying not to pull away. He took the strip around her hand again, then fastened it at her wrist, well away from the burned area. Silently she offered him her right hand. That looked even worse but she let him bandage it without a murmur.

'It looks nastier than it is,' said Ben, not knowing if that was true or not. 'This will keep the skin moist anyhow.'

He had just finished fastening the makeshift bandages when a shrill sound made him jump out of his skin.

He scanned the instruments, looking for a flashing red light or a whirling dial. 'What the hell is it? What's gone wrong?'

Kelly shook her head. 'It's just my phone.' She nodded towards the cradle by the instrument panel.

Ben pressed answer and the display flashed up the word 'Dad'.

It was a bad connection. In the middle of a lot of hissing and crackling, Ben could hear a male voice with an American accent.

'*Kelly . . . Kelly – you there? Are you all right? Tell me you're safe.*'

'Hi, Dad, I'm here. I'm safe. No problem. But are you all right?' Kelly reassured her dad – but clearly needed to know that he, too, was clear of any fire.

There was a hiss of static, then one phrase came through clearly. 'Protestors grabbed me . . .' More static.

'What?' said Kelly. 'Dad, can you repeat that?'

'*Protestors grabbed me . . .*'

They weren't sure the first time what he had said, but this time there was no mistaking it.

'Dad!' shouted Kelly. 'Are you all right?'

The major didn't answer Kelly's question; just went on talking. Maybe he couldn't hear them. Among the waves of hiss, only a few words were audible: '*Bel . . . conference centre . . .*'

Ben was shocked. He leaned close to the phone in its cradle, as if that would help the major hear him better. 'Bel? What about Bel? My mum – is she all right?'

Kelly leaned forward too. In fact it made no difference because the sound was going through the headset system. 'Dad, where are you?'

'Major Kurtis, where's Bel?'

'*I'm on the gan . . .*'

'Where?'

The connection was getting worse. The major tried once more. '*On the gan . . .*'

Then the connection failed and they heard no more.

Kelly waved her bandaged hands at the phone. 'Quick, call him back.'

Ben had the phone in his hands, trying to navigate the menu. 'I'm trying!' He found the major's number, but when he pressed call back, it wouldn't connect.

Kelly was frantic. 'Damn! I saw those protestors

this morning. I knew they were up to no good. They just hate Americans – we're an easy target. We lived near Sydney for a couple of years and had to have special security at home because somebody tried to fire-bomb our garden.' Suddenly she looked sharply ahead. 'Watch your altitude! We've drifted down three hundred feet!'

All at once Ben remembered the plane. He opened the throttle and climbed to fifteen hundred feet again.

Kelly snapped out more corrections. 'You're not level. And slow down, we're going to run out of fuel if you keep going like this. Have you any idea where we're heading?'

Ben was struggling to keep up with her instructions. 'No, I don't know where we're going. You were find-ing us somewhere to land. Just chill.'

Kelly spluttered. 'Chill? They've got your mom too – aren't you worried?'

'Of course I'm worried but we won't get anywhere by panicking. Is the plane OK? Can I leave it for long enough to call her?'

Kelly looked at the controls. 'Yeah. For a minute or so.'

Ben put his phone in the cradle and tried Bel. But it wouldn't make the connection.

'Call nine-one-one,' said Kelly.

'Treble zero,' said Ben irritably. He dialled and was put through immediately.

'*Which service do you require?*'

'Police.'

Another voice came on the line almost immediately. '*Hello, police here.*'

Kelly took over. 'My father is Major Brad Kurtis of the US army. He's just been kidnapped from the conference centre in Adelaide.'

'*Your father has been kidnapped?*' repeated the police controller. '*Are you sure?*'

'Yes, and there's someone with him. Dr Bel Kelland. She's British.'

'*Sorry, can you repeat that?*'

Ben took over. He spelled out Bel's name and tried to give a brief description. 'She's small, about five three, with red hair—'

Kelly interrupted, yelling, 'The gan! He said he was on the gan!'

Ben wanted to strangle her. She wasn't helping by

141

getting so hyper, and if she kept interrupting, how would the police ever get the information they needed?

'*Can you repeat that?*' asked the police controller patiently.

'G-H-A-N,' spelled out Kelly. She was reading off the map on her knee. Down one side was an advert with a picture of a big red train. 'It's a train that runs from Adelaide to Darwin.'

'*Oh yes,*' said the police controller. '*We know the Ghan. We'll send officers to investigate. Thank you for your call.*'

Kelly looked up at the fuel gauge and screwed up her face.

'What's the matter?' said Ben. 'Tell me what to do.'

'I'm working out if we've got enough fuel.'

'Why? Are we going to run out?'

Kelly did some silent calculations before she answered him. 'No. We've got plenty. We're going to follow the Ghan.'

Further down the coast, in Melbourne, the weather reporting station was hosting a crisis meeting. The mayor, the police chief and the head of the Melbourne fire department were gathered in the tiny office of the chief meteorologist discussing whether they should put their city on alert.

The meteorologist was pointing to a series of satellite images of Adelaide showing how the fire had progressed. In the final one, taken a couple of minutes earlier, the entire landscape was black, blotted out by clouds of smoke.

The fire chief spoke first: 'This fire should not be this bad. It should have been containable.'

His comment sent ripples of surprise through the cramped room.

'I agree,' said the meteorologist. 'Let me show you . . .' She cursored back, looking for a picture. 'It seems to have got dramatically worse when the weather changed.' She pointed out the features on the screen – the distinctive coastline of Adelaide. 'This is Port Adelaide here, the Murray river – we can see by the cloud formations that it's a hot, still day. The anemometers around the city confirm it; hardly any breeze at all.'

The fire chief pointed to some dark smudges on the

picture. 'You can see there are a few bush fires, but look at the smoke – they're not going anywhere. They would burn out safely if they were managed properly.'

The meteorologist took up the story. 'But now, if we look at this . . .' She scrolled along to another picture. 'This was ten minutes later.'

The audience gasped. The clouds had become black and white streaks swirling in an angry vortex. It looked like a picture of a hurricane.

'It must be some mistake,' said the police chief. 'It can't be the same day.'

'That's what I thought,' said the meteorologist. 'But there's no mistake. From nowhere we've got winds of up to a hundred k.p.h. When those winds blew up, that's when the fire really took hold.'

The chief of police sighed. 'Why didn't the fore-casters give us any warning of this?'

The meteorologist shook her head. 'They didn't know it was coming.'

The mayor looked incredulous. 'A wind can't just spring up out of nowhere. We've got half a billion dollars worth of satellite equipment to track this kind of thing!'

The meteorologist replied calmly, 'I agree with you. Something like that doesn't just sneak up unannounced. That's why I looked at the records myself. I looked at the exact same information the Adelaide forecasters had and I ran a computer simulation. And I came to the same conclusion as they did – that it would be a hot, still day.'

The mayor folded his arms. He looked very unhappy. 'So it's another spell of freak weather? We seem to be getting rather a lot of that.'

'We normally try to think in more scientific terms than that,' replied the chief meteorologist, 'but there's no explanation for this. We don't know why the weather changed. But when it did, it meant nothing short of disaster for Adelaide.'

Someone else was also taking a keen interest in weather satellite pictures of Adelaide. In a lab far more spacious than the monitoring station in Melbourne, two military scientists were looking closely at a screen, squinting to see it in the bright sunshine that streamed in through the window. They wore faded blue uniforms; the name tag on one said

GRISHKEVICH, the other's said HIJKOOP. Around them was a bank of computer monitors and electronic equipment, all emblazoned with the insignia of the US army. On racks of machinery around the walls, red and green LEDs flashed a constant pulse like heart-beat monitors, and glowing digital displays counted up and down. Whatever was going on in that room was very complex and needed expert monitoring.

Outside the window was a stretch of reddish desert criss-crossed by tyre marks, but the skyline was dominated by a massive white dome. A military Jeep was driving around the outside of that dome. It was probably doing about 50 k.p.h. – the speed limit within the compound – but the dome was so huge that the vehicle looked like it was hardly moving at all.

Beyond the dome was a high wire fence topped with barbed wire, which marked the perimeter of the compound; and beyond that was the Great Victoria Desert – a barren plain in the middle of the outback.

'Koop,' said Grishkevich, 'could you close those blinds? I can't see the screen properly.'

Hijkoop got up and pulled the blinds shut.

'Oh no,' said Grishkevich.

The tone in his voice made Hijkoop hurry back to look at what was on the screen. He was horrified by what he saw there.

Adelaide was completely blotted out by black clouds of smoke. Something had gone very wrong.

'I thought you were trying to up the rainfall, Grish,' said Hijkoop.

'Yeah.' Grishkevich let out a long sigh and ran his fingers through his thinning hair. 'No good. All we're getting is the wind speed picking up instead.'

Hijkoop couldn't take his eyes off the picture on the screen. 'Grish, we have to shut it down. The wind is going to make matters worse.'

Grishkevich shook his head slowly. Eventually he spoke. 'I already did shut it down. But I've got a nasty feeling it may be too late for that. Unless that wind dies down of its own accord, Adelaide's going to turn into a fire storm.'

Chapter Thirteen

Ben kept the microlight heading north. Down below, the railway line snaked through the desert. It was a relief to get away from the terrible burning landscape of Adelaide. But what they were seeing now was eerie.

The hills and foliage had given way to barren red desert. Ben had thought it was hot enough back in Adelaide, but now it was baking. They had already drunk half the water from Ben's remaining bottle. Kelly's bandages had nearly dried out and they had to use some of the water to soak them again. But at least the flying was easier. Because the terrain was so flat, there were fewer thermals and variations in the air currents. Ben hadn't had to adjust his altitude as often.

Which was just as well, as Kelly had him constantly pressing redial on the phone, trying to get her father's number again. The response came through, same as before: '*Lines are busy. Please try again later.*' Ben had lost count of the number of times he had heard that message. He got the same message whenever he called Bel's number.

Kelly tried a different tactic. 'Get me directory enquiries.'

Ben goggled at her. 'What did your last slave die of? Get it yourself.'

Kelly let out an irritated sigh. 'Ben, can you please dial directory enquiries. Please. Pretty please with swirly sparkly—'

'Maybe,' said Ben, 'if you tell me what you want it for.'

'I wanna get my nails done,' snapped Kelly. 'What does it matter what I want it for? You'll find out in a minute anyway.'

Ben smiled. 'Want to look nice for George?' He keyed in the number, which he remembered seeing in the hotel information leaflet. 'Directory enquiries coming right up for you, miss.'

Kelly scowled at him. When the call was answered, she spoke into the speaker. 'Hi,' she said. 'Can I get the US consulate in Melbourne? . . . Yes, please put me through – thank you.'

Ben listened, fascinated. The US consulate now? This girl certainly liked to pull out the big guns.

'Hello,' said Kelly. 'I'd like to report the kidnapping of a US citizen in Adelaide. He's Major Brad Kurtis.'

While she talked, Ben looked out of the window. A lone truck moved across the plain below, coated in so much red dust that it looked like it was camouflaged. The only reason Ben could see it was because of the puff of red dust following behind it. Even the road was barely visible. There was no asphalt, just the dusty red earth.

The railway line was a single track too. Big square water butts stood on stilts next to the signal. The plane passed over a point where the line split into two for a while to create a passing place if one train met another coming in the opposite direction. There was no sign of any train.

Kelly nudged Ben with her elbow. 'Watch the compass.'

'I thought we were following the railway line. Why do I need to watch the compass too?'

'What if it's not the right railway line? You don't forget about your compass or ignore any of your other instruments. Ever. You've got to be really careful out here because there are no landmarks and you could lose your way. That's why you've got instruments. Pay attention to them!'

A female voice with an American accent said: '*Excuse me?*' The woman at the US consulate had also received Ben's telling-off.

'Not you,' said Kelly. 'Yes, I've informed the police. And there's a British woman who's gone missing too. I don't know if you can do anything about that.'

'*Ma'am, if the local police are dealing with it, there is nothing else we can do.*'

'Oh,' said Kelly, taken aback. 'OK, thanks. You have a nice day too. Bye.'

Ben cut the call. Kelly looked out of the window for a moment, thinking. Ben looked at his instruments and suddenly saw they'd dropped to nine hundred feet. He pointed the nose upwards and pulled back on the throttle. Maybe he could correct it without Kelly noticing.

But she seemed to have eyes in the back of her head. 'What's your altitude?'

Ben winced. 'Um – I'm just sorting that out. Chill.'

Kelly was not to be appeased so easily. 'That's because you were flying looking at the ground. If you keep looking at the ground all the time, do you know what will happen? You'll end up there. Crashed. Finito. When planes crash, it isn't funny. You don't walk away. Do I have to spoon-feed you the entire time?'

'Look,' said Ben, 'I know you're frustrated because you'd rather be flying yourself, but you're not helping.' He dialled Bel's number – not because he thought the call would get through this time, but because he needed a break from Kelly's ranting.

But it was answered straight away.

'*Hello? Help! Help!*' The voice was high and anxious, almost screaming.

'Mum? Is that you?' Ben was horrified. Bel was so calm and controlled. He'd never known her lose her cool, ever. 'Mum, where are you? I'll get you out, where are you?'

'*Billy, is that you?*'

The woman had an Australian accent. It wasn't Bel. Somehow, even with speed-dial, he'd got a wrong number. An error in the computer switching at the exchange, he supposed. It must be overloaded.

Now that the woman had got through to someone, she poured out her troubles. '*I'm trapped in the flat. There are eight of us here. Rikki from next door. Old Mr Green from the ground floor – he's having trouble breathing.*' The voice shook. She sounded near to tears. '*We can't get through to the fire department . . . We daren't go downstairs.*'

Kelly looked at Ben, just as appalled as he was. In the background they could hear several voices all talking at once, suggesting more things to say. Kelly and Ben caught snatches of what they were saying. '*Other buildings on fire . . . lower floors full of smoke . . . Near the racecourse . . .*'

The racecourse.

Kelly looked at Ben. 'They're in Adelaide. By that racecourse.'

'I'm sorry,' said Ben into the phone. 'I'm not Billy. I'm Ben and I'm looking for my mum. But tell me where you are and I'll try to send help.'

'*What? You're breaking up . . .*'

The rest of her words dissolved in a flurry of static. The woman's voice had gone.

'Try and get her back,' said Kelly. 'Tell her we'll help if we can.'

Ben was pressing redial, but they got the same message as before. '*Lines are busy. Please try again later.*' He tried 000 to see if he could get help to them, but even that was unavailable.

'It must have been a fluke,' said Ben. 'The chances of getting her again are minimal.'

Kelly was quiet for a moment. 'I'm glad my dad isn't in Adelaide. I'd rather he got kidnapped than be trapped like that poor woman. Your mother too.'

Two police helicopters took off from Melbourne and skimmed out into the dusty red desert. They located the railway line that led out of Adelaide and began to follow it. The burning sky lay behind; ahead was the vast desert that formed the interior of the great continent of Australia, the Red Centre.

The Ghan was a big red train with a history, a tourist attraction like the Orient Express in Europe. It followed a 2,979-kilometre route that stretched right across the country from Adelaide in the south to Darwin in the north, a route originally established when Afghan camel trains trekked the parched outback.

After twenty minutes the lead helicopter spotted the train, sending up a plume of deep red dust like a vapour trail. They matched its speed and radioed the train controller to ask him to stop. As the train braked, they positioned themselves at the front and the back, hovering like hawks so that they had maximum visibility in case anyone left the train.

The train came to a standstill, throwing up clouds of dust like an old-fashioned steam engine and the helicopters came in to land.

Passengers leaned out of the windows, squinting into the sun. They were mystified to see the police boarding their train.

One group of officers searched the carriages. A

small squad stayed outside in case the kidnappers jumped off the train. If they did, they would be caught quickly as there was nowhere to hide here in the vast emptiness of the outback.

The officers searched the interior of the train twice, including all the nooks and crannies that only the train staff knew about. But no one answering the description of Bel or the major was on board.

The officers returned to their helicopters and radioed back to control. They had to get back to the burning skies of Adelaide.

Sixty kilometres to the south, unaware that the train had already been searched and their parents were not aboard after all, Ben and Kelly were risking the last of their fuel flying to intercept it.

The fire in Adelaide was spreading. Wanasri and the crew of Engine 33 watched the paramedics load a woman on a stretcher into the back of an ambulance and close the doors. The air was full of damp smoke and it was impossible to see more than a few hundred metres down the road. Wanasri's ears were ringing with the constant clamour of sirens, shouting, and the hiss of high-pressure water blasting from hoses. Every surface she touched was hot and wet. The streets were slick with water and steaming like a jungle.

Petra pulled open the cab of the truck and climbed into the driving seat. 'We're needed down the road. There are some people trapped inside a house.'

Wanasri, Andy and Darren didn't even bother to get back in the engine. They jogged down the road after Petra.

Wanasri stepped aside as the ambulance slalomed past, its siren wailing. Its fog lights were on so that it could navigate through the black clouds of smoke. It had a long journey ahead. The general hospital in the middle of town, which housed the major burns unit, was being evacuated, so new patients were being taken to an army barracks up the coast, which had set up an emergency medical centre. A small fire truck followed the ambulance, just in case. The crew drove with the windows up to keep out stray sparks. Muffled inside their heavy fireproof jackets, they looked like decontamination workers. The ambulance carried flammable materials like oxygen, which in this heat was like a cargo of nitroglycerine.

As Wanasri jogged along beside Darren and Andy, she kept thinking about the woman in that ambulance. They had rescued her from the fire but she had burns over most of her body. Her bare arms and legs were blistered and charred. Burns normally caused excruciating pain, but she seemed to feel no pain at all. At the time it seemed merciful, but Wanasri and the medics knew it was an ominous sign. When burns victims were quiet like that, it meant their nerve endings had been destroyed. They might lose limbs or die.

The injuries they were seeing today were getting worse as the fire grew further out of control.

Maybe with this next call, thought Wanasri, they would find somebody alive and well, or less severely injured. Maybe that pall of smoke they were heading towards would not contain the ashes of another unlucky victim.

As they got closer, her heart sank. It was a single-storey home. The roof had already collapsed and only part of a wall and a chimney remained. Another crew had put out most of the fire, but small hot spots still smouldered.

Andy and Darren reached the truck and unclipped pike poles – long fibreglass poles with hooks on the end for lifting hot materials. With a heavy heart Wanasri reached for hers. She felt a tap on her shoulder.

A woman was standing behind her. Tears made clean tracks down her soot-smudged face. 'I'm the landlady,' she said. I live two doors down. The tenant who lives here is blind. You've got to find him.'

Wanasri nodded. 'Ma'am,' she replied, 'it's not safe for you to be here. There are a lot of unstable structures. You just stay there, and we'll look for your tenant, right?'

The woman looked so bewildered; maybe she just wanted to be told what to do.

Andy and Darren had their pike poles hooked into the corners of the roof. They started to push, lifting the roof away from the door so that they could get inside. Smoke gushed out – it was like taking the lid off a boiling saucepan; then hot embers, starved of oxygen when the roof fell on them, began to stir into flame again. Petra followed the others with a hose line and shot water at the flames until they disappeared.

Wanasri stepped carefully across the blackened debris to join the others. It was slippery, like crossing rocks at low tide. She steadied herself with her pike pole. The smoke and steam were clearing and the debris began to take shape. She identified the frame of a sofa, all the upholstery gone.

Now that she had met the landlady, she wanted more than ever to find the blind man safe and well. Hoping against hope, she began to think of reasons why he might be all right. The people who died in house fires were often simply disorientated by the smoke and couldn't find their way out, even if they'd lived in the same place for twenty years. But perhaps someone who was used to finding his way around with senses other than sight would have a better chance.

She reached Andy and helped him lift up a beam. Andy looked under it, then stopped.

Wanasri knew that expression; even the most seasoned firefighters couldn't help but react when they found a body. She caught a glimpse of teeth glinting white in the smoking black wreckage and looked away quickly. 'Is that him?'

Andy shook his head. 'It's not human. It must be the guide dog.'

He didn't have to say any more. Animals usually managed to get out more easily than humans did; they were faster and smaller. If the dog hadn't got out, the owner definitely hadn't. The body was definitely here somewhere.

Wanasri felt a lump rising in her throat. She had a dog. She'd had him for just a few months and already they were devoted to each other. She couldn't bear to think of such a horrible death befalling such a trusting companion. How could this day get any worse?

The landlady had seen them and was walking shakily over the wreckage towards them. 'Go and head her off,' said Andy. 'She doesn't need to see this.'

Bel was walking through a blackened, smoky, steaming hell. She was in a paved precinct. She didn't know where she was going, she just wanted to find a safe place to stop. There were shops on either side but they were burned out. Their blackened signs dripped with water. The paving slabs were cracked where heavy fire trucks had driven along them. Sun umbrellas lay on the ground like felled trees, the fabric burned away; café tables and chairs were flattened. It looked like the fire brigade had swept in, blasted the whole lot and swept away all the people with it too. Was she completely alone?

She passed a shop and realized that the strange shape standing in the window was vaguely human. As Bel went closer, the heat suddenly shattered the plate-glass window. It cobwebbed with cracks and then exploded out into the street, showering her with glass. Smoke billowed out, blinding and choking her.

In the midst of the smoke stood the human figure. It had its arms up towards her. And it was melting . . .

That tripped a switch in her brain. She screamed and ran towards a square of parched grass beyond the precinct. Here she fell to her knees: she couldn't run any further. Her lungs were burning and she couldn't get any oxygen. She stayed there on her hands and knees, gasping. Gradually, common sense began to return. The melting figure must have been a mannequin. All this smoke and heat must be playing tricks with her head. She would give anything to breathe some cool, clear air.

She looked down. Her eyes were watering, blurring her vision, but she couldn't make sense of what she was seeing. She had assumed she was kneeling on grass, but instead it seemed to be a mass of strange shapes and colours: browns and blacks and reds. Was she in the middle of a flowerbed? She blinked several times, trying to work out what it was.

As her vision settled, she saw that the blobs were moving.

She felt something run over her hand. Looking down, she saw a grey blob of hair. Long furry legs stretched out from the blob and a tiny pair of pinpoint eyes looked out over a pair of pulsing mandibles.

It was a huntsman spider – the legs were longer than her fingers. And it had company. Those other strange shapes around her were more spiders, cockroaches, giant caterpillars and other huge insects . . . and rats.

The entire square of grass was covered in these creatures. Driven from the surrounding buildings and sewers by the heat, they'd all ended up on this one patch of damp grass.

Bel screamed and jumped to her feet. The spider fell

off her hand; she didn't see where it landed. She stepped backwards, felt something crunch under her feet, then caught a glimpse of yellow innards under the toe of her sandal and leaped back in disgust.

Something was tickling her bare leg. A caterpillar, nearly as long as her hand, was rippling over her ankle. It had green stripes and black hair and was twice as thick as the strap of her shoe. She shook her leg violently, then froze as she remembered the caterpillars were just as likely to be poisonous as the spiders. The caterpillar tumbled to the ground.

She started to pick her way back to the pavement. Every step she took, she felt feelers and legs and bristles. Her strappy sandals gave no protection – she might as well not have been wearing shoes at all. There was a lawnmower standing on the patch of grass, and the caterpillars and spiders were swarming all over it. She nearly tripped and her heart turned a complete somersault. She imagined herself sprawled on the ground, the creatures crawling all over her. Bel had a strong stomach, but this much poisonous antipodean wildlife was enough to unsettle even her.

A deafening noise in the sky made her look up. The

silver underbelly of an airliner flashed above the rooftops. It was close enough for her to see the red and white lights on its wings, and the winged insignia of the Royal Australian Air Force. Why was it flying so low? And in such difficult conditions? It must be at barely five hundred feet.

Her flyer's instinct told her that the plane was in trouble. No pilot would bring a big plane like that in so low, particularly near buildings.

If the airliner came down on the town, the destruction would be terrible. All that aviation fuel would be like spraying a bonfire with gasoline.

A hatch opened in the plane's underbelly. Were people baling out?

Suddenly a wall of water slammed into her: it was as if several inches of rainfall had all come down in a split second. She was knocked off her feet. When she got up again, the smoky air had turned to steam and she was soaked to the skin.

She looked up. The water was such a relief in the heat. All around her, the pavements and the buildings were hissing. Even better, Bel realized the grass around her was clear. The water had driven all those dreadful creatures away. She imagined them swept into the gutters, their furry legs and feelers twitching helplessly. Her heart suddenly leaped. Was it a tropical storm? Was this nightmare ending at last? A storm would do the trick. She turned her face up to the skies, expecting to feel rain on her skin.

But there was no rain. There was only the plane, climbing now into the dark sky, disappearing into the clouds of smoke.

Bel understood. The pilot's reckless flight pattern made sense now. The plane had dropped the water – the equivalent of the contents of a small plunge pool. Now the plane was climbing again, soaring away into the smoky black sky. Moments later she heard another gigantic splash followed by a hiss as it dropped another load.

She waited to see if the water would help clear the black pall of smoke, but it didn't. It was going to take a lot more water than that to stop the city burning. But rain seemed like a dream on a swelteringly dry day like this. Bel didn't believe in God, but she had never been more tempted to try a prayer just for luck.

She had reached the edge of the green and could see

an outdoor activities shop. Its front window was broken but it seemed to have escaped the flames. She got up and strode purposefully towards it. It was time she got some boots. Her sandal-wearing days were behind her, she decided.

As she walked, she took her phone out and tried to call Ben. She couldn't get through. After a few tries she had to give up. It was hardly surprising. There were probably a half million other people all trying to place calls at the exact same moment.

Bel put the phone back in her pocket. Where was Ben? Had he managed to land somewhere safely?

How would she ever find him again in all this chaos?

Chapter Fourteen

In the desert below, the railway line snaked up to a small cluster of buildings. 'I can see a station,' said Ben. 'And a couple of huts.'

Kelly consulted the map on her knee. 'It's Coober Pedy.'

'I think we should land,' Ben said. 'We can ask if the police have found my mum or your dad.'

Kelly mulled over the idea, biting her lip. She seemed reluctant.

'If we don't land here,' said Ben, 'how far are we going to go? All the way to Darwin?'

Kelly straightened up in her seat. 'OK, give me control. I might be able to land.'

Ben was surprised she was going to try it. He was a bit disappointed too. He felt he had got the hang of flying and was looking forward to trying a landing. With a sigh he took his hands away. Kelly reached for the controls.

As soon as her left hand touched the stick her mouth twisted with pain. She folded her arms into her body, hunching over them protectively.

'No good. My hands are too painful,' she gasped.

'That's another reason for landing. There ought to be a doctor around here.'

'One station building and two huts? You're being optimistic.'

Ben shrugged. 'At least they'd have a proper first-aid kit. Look, can you talk me through landing?'

Kelly thought about it. Instead of answering, she said, 'You've got control.'

'I've got control.' Ben took back the stick and the throttle. He felt a bit guilty, but all the same he was pleased to get the chance.

Kelly straightened up. 'Landing is the most dangerous part of flying and it's difficult. You've got to do exactly as I say.'

Ben gave her a withering look. She certainly knew how to wipe out any ounce of sympathy he might feel. 'Do I ever not do as I'm told?'

Kelly looked out of the window. 'Let your altitude drop to five hundred feet. We'll aim for that flat stretch of road there, so bring her around in a big circle while I check it out.'

Ben tilted the stick left and balanced with a little rudder. He executed a perfect turn to the left, then glanced at the altimeter. It said eight hundred feet. He now felt completely at home manoeuvring the little craft in the air. Landing would be a cinch. He put the nose down.

'That's too steep!' shrieked Kelly. 'We're going too fast. Ease off the throttle and that'll take you lower. You don't need to point the nose down.'

A bit shocked at being shouted at, Ben pushed the throttle down to decrease the revs.

'Not too slow! You might stall. Don't let the speed get below fifty knots.'

'All right,' Ben retorted through gritted teeth. 'No need to screech about it.'

'Throttle!' she said.

In a moment, thought Ben, I might throttle you.

Kelly looked out of the window again.

'What are you looking for?' said Ben. 'I thought you'd decided where to land.'

'I'm checking to see how bumpy it is. And that there are no obstacles like trees or telegraph poles.'

Ben glanced out of the other side. All he could see was a few scrubby buildings: a shed and a petrol station with a dust-encrusted flag hanging limply on a flagpole, then the railway station a little way away. 'Don't be daft, there's nothing for miles.'

'Yes, well, I'm telling you how to do it properly. Making assumptions can get you killed. Right, there's no wind and we're at five hundred feet. Keep that height and fly over the path you will take, just to check everything is safe.'

Ben turned and took the microlight over the makeshift runway at exactly five hundred feet. He remembered to check the plane was level.

'That's good,' said Kelly. 'Go round to the start again, and as you go, point the nose down – just a touch – so we descend.'

Ben could tell by her voice that this was it. Butterflies were building up in his stomach.

By the time they reached the start of the runway, they were at two hundred feet.

After spending so long seeing only sky on each side of him, it was rather disconcerting to see the ground so close.

'Turn here,' said Kelly. 'We're going to land.'

One hundred feet. The runway was ahead of them, taking up nearly half the windscreen. Their speed was 60 knots. The butterflies in Ben's stomach clumped together in an uncomfortable lump. 60 knots felt rather fast. The ground shot past underneath them. Would that spindly undercarriage take it?

'Put the nose down just a touch more,' said Kelly. 'Close the throttle down gently. We want to be slow – fifty knots – but we don't want to stall. You're going to continue coming down like this then put the heels down and she'll land.'

Ben eased closer to the ground. He saw small rocks whizzing past and felt all his confidence draining away fast.

'Put the nose down more,' said Kelly. 'And don't

look at the ground, look ahead or it will all come up too quickly.'

Ben looked ahead. As he did so, a kangaroo hopped into the road, stopped and sat on its haunches.

Ben looked at Kelly in alarm. 'Where's the horn?'

'Pull up!' yelled Kelly. 'If we hit it, we're toast!'

Ben opened the throttle again. The engine roared. The kangaroo blinked at them, then the view changed to deep blue sky again.

Kelly leaned out of the window as the microlight soared upwards. 'Stupid thing's still sitting there. Come round again and we'll land to one side of it.'

Ben's heart was pounding. The aborted landing had really shaken him. His mind went blank. 'What do I do?'

'Ease off the throttle and bring her down.'

Ben did as he was told.

They came round again. 'Get straight and level,' said Kelly. 'Then point the nose down until I tell you to bring it up.'

The kangaroo was still sitting on their runway, blinking at them gormlessly. At this altitude it looked like a man in an oversize rabbit suit.

'Don't you dare move, Skippy,' said Ben. Sweat trickled down inside his suit.

'Don't look at the stupid kangaroo,' said Kelly. 'Look where you're going! Right, you're at thirty feet – ease the nose up – slowly. Keep her level, you're wobbling. We don't want to touch down with one wheel. Just relax.'

Relax? When he was sitting here being bombarded by instructions? When the ground was whizzing past only metres away? His hands were so slippery with sweat that he could barely keep his grip on the stick.

'Bring the nose back a bit more.'

Ben tweaked the stick back.

'Not that much! We'll stall! Nose forward—'

Too late. There was a bang which Ben felt all the way up to his teeth. They were on the ground.

'Throttle off!' yelled Kelly. 'Brakes on!' She leaned forward with her arms folded, her hands tucked protectively by her elbows. Wasn't that what airlines told you to do for an emergency landing?

Ben squeezed the brake handle. The craft slowed. Slowly he let out his breath. He seemed to have it under control. A huge grin spread across his face. 'Wow, I got us down!'

Slowly Kelly straightened up. 'Yeah, and you nearly took our undercarriage off doing it. Taxi over to the station there. Let's find out what's going on.'

'How do I do that?'

'Just drive it like a car. Steer it with the stick and the pedals. But keep the stick forwards so the nose is down.'

Ben hadn't driven a car before of course, but he reckoned he could guess what to do. The station was a single-storey shack like a couple of Portakabins and a big water butt, and it was about two hundred metres away, so he pulled the throttle up to work up some speed. But he did it too much. The microlight shot forward at 70 knots, the engine howled and the rpm needle swung into the red.

'Not that fast!'

'Oops,' said Ben, and slowed to 40 knots. It was an uncomfortable ride: they felt every bump in the ground. Steering felt different on the ground too and it took Ben a few goes to get it right. The kangaroo blinked at them as they bumped towards the station in a series of S shapes.

Finally Ben braked and unclipped his seat belt.

'Set the parking brake and cut the engine,' said Kelly.

Ben did as he was told and slipped open the catch on his door. 'I'll let you out from the other side.'

Kelly shook her head. 'I'll stay here. You go and ask.'

Her face was trickling with sweat. Ben's was too, but he didn't think it was just the heat in Kelly's case. She was hunched over her hands again, protecting them.

He put his phone into the pocket of his flying suit, disconnected his headset and slipped it round his neck, and jumped out.

Away from the shade of the plane, the sun was mercilessly hot. Ben unzipped his flying suit. Underneath, his T-shirt was soaked with sweat. The dust stuck to his arms and face.

He walked into the station building. Two big fans rotated in the ceiling but they barely stirred the air. A pair of double doors led to the railway track. There was just one platform. It looked like only half a station. Obviously the northbound and southbound trains never arrived at the same time.

'G'day.' The stationmaster pushed open the door of

the ticket office. He was a robust-looking man in his sixties with a peaked cap and a shirt in the red livery of the Ghan.

'Hi,' said Ben.

The man looked out of the window at the parked microlight. 'That's a stylish way to travel. I'd stick to that if I were you; faster than the train. Especially today – it's been delayed.'

'Why was it delayed?' said Ben.

'Kidnapping in Adelaide. That makes a change. We've been delayed by floods, lightning strikes and roos on the line, but never an attempted kidnapping. The police stopped it for half an hour.'

'Did they catch them?'

'No. Turned out to be a hoax or a false alarm.' The stationmaster shrugged. 'Still, makes a change.'

'Are you absolutely sure the police didn't find any-one on the train?' said Ben.

'Oh yes. They gave us the all-clear. They don't take any chances these days, what with terrorists and suchlike.'

Ben was stunned. Bel and the major hadn't been on the train after all. So where were they?

Through the open door to the ticket office Ben could see a drinks fridge. Condensation had collected on the window; the row of cans and bottles inside looked cool and inviting. He reached in his pocket for some coins. 'Can I buy a couple of bottles of water?'

'Sure.' The stationmaster went to the fridge. 'If you need to refuel, my sister runs the roadhouse next door.'

'Actually,' said Ben, 'can you tell me where the town is?'

The stationmaster brought two bottles over to Ben and made a sweeping gesture with his hand. 'This is the town. That's a dollar fifty.'

Ben paid him. Out of the window he could see the dusty petrol station, a few hills shaped like pyramids and a number of small sheds. The road was just a smoothing out of the desert texture. In the microlight, Kelly was waving her gold and black paws to shoo away a pair of emus who were strutting over to peck at the plane, but nothing else in the landscape moved.

'Sorry,' said Ben, 'I mean a big town. My friend needs a doctor.' He handed over some coins.

The stationmaster beckoned him over to a map on

the wall. He pointed to the railway station with a stubby finger. 'You're right here.'

On the map, the station was in the centre of a complex array of streets: a church, a motel, a school, a theatre. It didn't correspond with the isolated shacks that Ben saw out of the window.

The stationmaster chuckled. 'Son, we not only have a doctor, we have a hospital. In fact, you're parked on top of it. Welcome to Coober Pedy.'

'I don't understand,' said Ben, beginning to think that the poor old guy must have gone doolally in the heat.

'The town,' said the stationmaster. 'It's all built under the ground.'

Chapter Fifteen

In Adelaide, the streets were full of boiling smoke. The police and ambulances were busy dealing with casualties; the fire brigade had their hands full trying to deal with the fires. The army had organized mass evacuations, but so many people slipped through the net – the ones who hadn't got out fast enough, or were stuck somewhere that was inaccessible.

Those people were now trying to get to safety by themselves.

Some made good decisions, others didn't. It was impossible to tell which option would be more dangerous until you tried it. Whether you survived was more down to luck than judgement. Choices had to be made in a split second. Do you open this door or that door? Do you run down this road or that road? Every choice was a toss of the coin. Heads you win, tails you lose.

Victoria and Troy had so far made the right decisions. They fled from the golf course, not knowing where they were going. They came out onto a road they'd never seen before, lined with burning houses. The sky was dark and full of strange smells. Halfway down the road Victoria noticed some white gates on fire and realized she knew the street very well: she'd cycled up it every day for the past five months and fantasized about living in the big house behind those gates.

They reached the end of the road and chose to turn right. They didn't know it, but they'd won another coin toss. If they'd gone the other way, they would have been under the burning telegraph pole as it collapsed across the street.

When they reached the corner shop, they had to stop running – there was too much smoke and they couldn't breathe.

Ahead of them, a car exploded, vaporizing into a ball of mangled steel and burning petrol.

That was another coin toss won. If they had continued running, they would have been caught in the blast.

They darted down an alleyway and came out in a small precinct on the edge of the shopping area. For the first time, they saw some other people: a vet in green overalls and latex gloves; a decorator with smears of yellow and white paint on his clothes; a postman in his navy-blue uniform; a jockey from the racetrack, still in crash helmet and goggles, his candy-striped silks and breeches streaked with soot. Victoria and Troy felt reassured to see people who had come from the same part of town. The vet and the jockey felt the same when they saw Victoria and Troy in their golf shoes, eye shields and single gloves. To have got this far from the golf course and racetrack, they must have made good choices. Everybody hoped that luck was contagious – there was bound to be safety in numbers.

The group pressed on together towards the centre of town. Surely the fire wouldn't follow them there.

Surely concrete and brick buildings would give them more shelter than the woods and grass on the outskirts.

As they hurried on, burned-out restaurants and bars emerged from the smoke – then the casino, the building newer than the others and perhaps built from more fire-retardant materials. Certainly the windows still looked intact.

They approached the building and Victoria reached for the door handle. It was hot. She let go and herded the others away. Instinct told her it was burning inside.

Suddenly a green neon sign appeared through the smoke, flashing fitfully: SWIMMING POOL.

The jockey went ahead and pushed open the double doors. Inside, the turnstiles were open and the shimmering blue waters of the pool were visible at the end of a short corridor.

Water. That had to be safe. Another winning toss, it seemed.

They all ran in and headed for the corridor that led to the water.

All at once the vet began to cough. 'Stop!' she called. 'I can smell something.'

'It's just the chlorine from the pool,' said the jockey.

Victoria also started coughing and her eyes were watering. She never liked the smell of swimming pools but this seemed much worse than that.

Then the jockey was choking, and the decorator too. He put his hand on a door handle to steady himself and pulled it back sharply. 'It's hot—' His words ended in another spasm of coughing.

It was Troy who recognized the smell. He pushed the decorator away from the door, back towards the turnstiles, and put his hand over his mouth to stop the fumes long enough to speak. 'Get out! That's the chemical store. I used to work at a spa. You have to keep the chemicals cool. If they get hot, they explode.'

The group spluttered their way back to the turnstiles and out into the street.

Another coin toss won.

Bel's lungs were raw and her eyes were watering. At least she had managed to get some Brasher walking boots from the outdoor shop on the green. She didn't like the idea of looting so she'd scribbled a note with her name and address and details of what she owed them.

She walked along, with no idea where she was going. She was just looking for somewhere to rest. But you couldn't shelter in burned-out shops. She'd been in fire-damaged streets after tsunamis and floods and she knew the dangers. Charred roof beams could give way. Cracked pipes leaked gas and toxic fumes.

Bel scanned the deserted side streets. Why were there no other people around? Had they all found places to hide? Had there been an evacuation which she'd somehow missed?

She had her mobile in her hand and she repeatedly speed-dialled Ben's number as she walked.

'*Lines are busy . . .*' squawked the tiny voice in her hand.

Well, of course they were. What did she expect? Of course there was no way she was going to get through.

As she put the phone away, she caught sight of her face in a shop window. It wore an expression she had seen thousands of times before. Not when she looked in her own bathroom mirror, but when she worked in disaster zones, when mothers and fathers were worrying about their loved ones. *I'm alive*, that expression said, *but what about the others in my family?*

Was Ben at the hotel? Had he tried to get into town? What if he had been up in the air? A microlight would be thrown about like a paper aeroplane in the thermals from a major fire. Even so, it was probably safer in the air than on the ground. She'd have to trust to Major Kurtis's daughter to bring him back in one piece.

Across the green, a neon sign appeared through the smoke. It flashed on and then off, as though the power supply was faulty. The first time Bel caught the flicker of light out of the corner of her eye, she thought her mind was playing tricks. But then the sign flashed again: SWIMMING POOL.

Relief flooded through her. An open-air pool would be the safest place to be right now.

She ran across the road and up the steps and pushed through the doors of the building.

Inside it was dark. A strong reek of chemicals wiped out the smell of smoke. It was hot in here, almost as hot as it was outside. Down a short corridor, a big rectangle of blue water shimmered in the gloom.

Bel wasn't looking for a covered pool. The risk there was that the roof might give way. But maybe there was an open-air pool at the back of the building. She headed on through.

She didn't take any notice of the store cupboard door she passed on her left – which meant she didn't notice the paint on it peeling in the intense heat on the other side. A steady stream of white smoke crept out under the door, covering the floor like a carpet.

Bel coughed as she became aware of a strong chemical reek. The sound echoed off the walls. She marvelled at how silent the building was. Normally at this time of day the building would ring with high-spirited screams and splashes. Goggles, shoes and bags littered the edge of the pool where swimmers had fled. She never got used to disaster zones – the deserted places, scattered with dropped possessions.

The corridor smelled strong – it was probably toxic, she thought. Fearing a chemical leak, she started to run, but her feet slipped on the wet floor and she fell sprawling.

The impact knocked all the wind out of her. When

she sucked in a breath, the white smoke drifting around at ground level stung her throat like acid. She felt as if she'd been sprayed in the face with tear gas.

Behind her there was a deafening bang. The door flew off its hinges and smacked into the tiled wall opposite, scattering broken chips of ceramic. Bel's vision cleared in time to see a ball of fire rolling towards her.

She flattened herself on the floor and started scuttling away all fours. The wet tiled surface was easy to move on and she slithered as fast as a fish. At the water's edge she just carried right on in and powered down the pool in a strong crawl.

She was a good swimmer but her new boots pulled her down like lead weights. When her hand touched the wall at the other end she gripped it gratefully and pulled herself up.

The corridor she had come down was now a mass of flames. Fire and thick black smoke boiled out of the store cupboard. She blinked back stinging tears and saw that the insulation in the ceiling tiles was starting to smoulder, like those in the conference centre.

The swimming pool was not a safe place to be. She had to get out.

She dragged herself out of the water, onto the tiled surround. Pain shot through her shoulder: she must have bruised it badly when she fell over. She got unsteadily to her feet and looked around.

There was a door to the men's changing rooms and another that seemed to go up to a viewing gallery. She went for the men's changing rooms. Her boots had filled with water and squelched heavily with every step. Her skirt stuck to her legs, bandaging them together. She stumbled and nearly fell again, all the time conscious of the smoke and fumes billowing into the air around her.

The changing rooms were a mess. People had obviously left in a hurry – clothes were strewn on the benches and floors. But smoke was curling out over the cubicles. She turned back. The more confined the space, the bigger the risk of being overcome by fumes. She had more chance in the large open area of the pool room.

She went up the steps to the gallery. Her clinging skirt made her take tiny, hobbling steps. She tried ripping it, but the wet fabric was stronger than it looked. There was no time to waste. Already thick white fumes were covering the surface of the pool. She stumbled on and saw that the fire escape door was open! She stepped out onto a metal walkway. It continued in a diagonal line across the roof, with railings on each side.

Bel looked down. Smoke filled the streets like dark cotton wool. Here and there emergency lights twinkled in blue and orange.

The iron handrail was hot under her hands. Was that from the ambient summer temperature or something else? A few metres away there was a skylight in the roof. Bel went over and looked into it. The blue water of the pool was barely visible. The room below was filling with smoke of two colours, swirling together like tornado clouds on a satellite photo – black from the fire and white from the fumes given off by the reacting pool chemicals. She had got out just in time.

And she couldn't stay up here.

She hurried along the gantry. There were other skylights, but she didn't stop to look down into them. If she had, she would have noticed that the last one wasn't positioned over the pool, but over a small room to one side. Five people lay in there, huddled together, their matching yellow T-shirts soaked in sweat.

Amy looked up as she saw a figure cross the skylight. She tried to call out but she was too weak. The fumes sapped her strength. Slowly she pulled herself over towards Timi. He was curled up as though asleep. The angry scowl was now replaced by a placid look. He had such a young face, Amy realized. He looked untroubled and innocent. She stroked his brow and he mumbled something. His eyelids fluttered but they didn't open.

She looked up at the skylight again. It seemed to be getting darker. Joseph raised his head and looked at her. 'I feel so sleepy, Ames . . .'

'It's all right, Joe,' she told him. He smiled and closed his eyes, trusting in her. Just like when they were kids.

Amy felt so calm. She believed her soul would be reborn. Death was only the start of another opportunity. Or maybe it was the fumes that made her so resigned. She wasn't sure, but she was grateful for it.

She had one stab of regret as the warm darkness folded its arms around her. The woman they had locked in the conference centre – Dr Kelland. Amy hoped she'd got out somehow before the fire . . .

Up on the roof, Bel didn't have any idea how close she had come to crossing paths with the Oz Protectors again. Like her, they had gone into the pool to shelter. And like her, they had found it was a bad choice. In their case, a fatal choice.

Bel, running down the iron fire escape into the street, had made the right call. For now.

Chapter Sixteen

Ben had been to a hospital casualty unit once in his life, when he had twisted his ankle skateboarding. But the hospital in Coober Pedy was nothing like Accident and Emergency at Macclesfield General. As Ben waited for Kelly to come back from the triage nurse, he wouldn't have been surprised if the Flintstones had walked in.

For a start, the hospital was ten metres underground and carved out of solid rock. Most of Coober Pedy's buildings were like this, fashioned out of old opal mines. Of course, there were no windows, so the only light came from lamps mounted at intervals along the walls. Wooden partitions sectioned off the casualty waiting area from the examination rooms. The floor seemed normal enough – just cool green lino – but when Ben looked up at the ceiling, it was disorienting to just see rough-hewn rock like the inside of a cave. There were ventilation shafts in the ceiling, covered by cones of blue plastic like upturned lampshades. Every so often the plastic cones made a skittering sound, as pebbles fell down from the surface. But at least the temperature down here was pleasantly cool.

The waiting room was quite busy. Ben found that surprising as he had hardly seen anyone on the streets above. But even more peculiar was the appearance of these patients. There were no arms in slings, or plaster casts, or even makeshift bandages like Kelly's. Instead, most of them were wearing dark glasses, or sitting with their hands shielding their eyes.

All of them were tanned but some looked chalky pale under their tan, as though they were about to be sick. One woman sitting near Ben was holding her head in her hands and rocking backwards and forwards, moaning. Another got up and rushed to the bathroom, banging through the door in her hurry. It seemed to Ben like they had arrived in the middle of some weird kind of epidemic.

Kelly came back, her hands encased in sterile plastic bags. She looked miserable as she sat down next to Ben. 'They haven't finished with me yet – they've given me some painkillers, and once those start to work they can finish dressing the wounds. Can you get me something to eat?'

Ben stood up. 'Sure. What do you want?'

'A sandwich. Anything. There's a café in the art gallery just down the road. And see if you can get some fuel. We'll never make it back to Adelaide on what we've got left.'

Ben followed the sign to the lift. The doors opened and a group of people got out – a woman in a wheel-chair, caked in outback dust, being pushed by a paramedic. A man followed behind, carrying a dark brown snake that he'd chopped in half. Blood dripped from the snake's body onto the floor. At least that looked like a normal reason to visit a hospital, but Ben shuddered. He remembered the leaflet he'd been given with all the warnings about poisonous insects and spiders and reptiles. The man must have brought the snake in to identify the venom. It could be a harsh world out here in the Australian desert.

The lift rattled upwards. As Ben went out into the street, the heat hit him like a fist. He could see why everyone lived underground here. Out of habit, he tried to call Bel on his mobile, and Major Kurtis on Kelly's, but he couldn't even get a signal.

He put the phones away and looked for the art gallery. He spotted its blackboard on a shed, next to a sign warning people not to walk backwards because of unmarked shafts. The shed door was open. Ben went in and down a steep staircase, into another cool, twilit cave.

At the bottom of the stairs was a rack of postcards and a sign pointing to the café. It was at the other end of the art gallery. Striplights ran along the wall, inviting the visitor into small caves of treasures. Ben glimpsed opals, brightly coloured paintings and big black and white photographs. But he was intent on reaching the café. As he smelled the aroma of baked bread, he quickened his pace. He hadn't realized until now how hungry he was.

A lady in a T-shirt and a green apron came out of a side room, sweeping up dust that had fallen from the ceiling. 'Can I help you?'

'Is the café open?' Ben asked her.

'No, but I can open it for you if you just want sandwiches.'

'That would be great,' said Ben.

She leaned the broom against the wall. 'I'll get the key. We've got cheese and ham – is that all right?'

'Fine,' said Ben. 'And do you have any water?'

'Sure. I'll give you a shout when it's ready. You carry on looking around.'

He wandered back down the passageway and into one of the caves. It was filled with large photographs of Coober Pedy when the mines were being created. He went into another alcove, where there was an image painted directly onto the rock. A sign said it was a reproduction of a piece of aboriginal dreamtime art about the formation of opals, in which a stone in the ground was filled with fire and the colours of the rainbow.

Fire. Ben wished he could find a radio with the news on. He wanted to know what was happening in

Adelaide. He came out into the main gallery and saw a payphone. He went over to it, slotted some coins in and tried Bel's number.

'*Lines are busy. Please try again later.*'

He put the receiver down and spotted a newspaper on the shelf in the phone booth. Ben doubted whether the newspapers would have got an edition out in the short time since the fire had started, but still he unfolded it and scoured it eagerly.

It was a local paper, the *Coober Pedy Times*. The front page headline was: MYSTERY ILLNESSES CONTINUE. Underneath, a smaller headline said: *Tormented by noises*. There was a picture of the stationmaster Ben had spoken to earlier.

Ben looked down the corridor at the kitchen. The café owner was taking a packet out of the fridge. He turned back to the paper.

Monty Allen, Coober Pedy's stationmaster, has enjoyed good health all his life, but in the past three weeks has been driven mad by an unexplained ailment. 'I was hearing this humming in my ears,' said Mr Allen, 63. 'It went on for hours and I couldn't sleep so I went to the doctor. He said he'd had a surgery full of people with the same problem that morning and he didn't know what had caused it.'

There was another story further down the page: *'Farmer loses twenty calves in a week – is mystery illness spreading to cattle?'*

Ben turned the page. There was a story about bizarre weather patterns: sudden hurricanes and hailstorms. Hailstorms, thought Ben – in this heat?

'Here you go. That's four dollars seventy.'

The café owner was standing in front of him, holding out a bag and a four-pack of water bottles. Ben dug into his pocket for more change and peered at the unfamiliar notes. He worked out he hadn't got enough and pulled some more out of his pocket.

As he did so, a roughly folded piece of paper fell onto the floor. The café owner picked it up and was about to hand it back to him when something caught her eye. 'Oh, is this from here?' She opened it out.

Ben recognized it as the photocopy the police officer had handed him, showing the charred leaflet.

'No,' he said, 'I got it in Adelaide.'

'*Depression, skin diseases, strange allergies, migraines . . .*' She skim-read the page, muttering some of the words out loud, then handed it back to Ben. 'My sister has had a migraine for three days and she's sitting in casualty right now. Last week I had this terrible itching. I thought my skin was crawling with insects. I went to the doctor. He said he'd seen ten cases but he didn't know what was causing it. So we're making headlines in Adelaide now, are we?'

Ben had assumed that most of the text was crackpot scaremongering, but now he wasn't so sure. He glanced at the photocopy in his hand. The headline he had noticed before leaped out:

STOP SECRET US EXPERIMENTS

In Adelaide the army had established base camps for firefighting crews all around the city. They meant that the firefighters could rest up, replenish supplies and refuel without having to go back to their station house.

Engine 33 was based at the golf course. Driving in

was like entering a military installation. There was a clearly defined perimeter, where soldiers in firefighting gear patrolled with water tanks on trolleys. They had already had to put out several minor blazes, ignited by sparks blown in on smoke from the burning town.

Inside the firebreak, the whole area looked chaotic: a mass of parked fire trucks and personnel in fire-fighting gear apparently milling about in all directions. But in fact it was tightly organized.

A soldier noted Engine 33's identification number and told Petra where to park. She drove past a group of soldiers: some were tinkering about with an engine, others were replacing used breathing gear, checking rescue harnesses and testing hoses. Another engine bumped down the fairway towards them, its crew refuelled and ready for action again. The other crew waved as they went past and Wanasri watched them in the wing mirror as they reached the exit. Just then a glow of orange flared in the blackened bushes at the perimeter. The soldiers on duty immediately spotted it and dowsed it with water.

Even here, the firefighters couldn't relax totally; the fire was never truly beaten. No matter how much water they hosed onto it, everything dried out so quickly in the blistering afternoon heat.

Petra turned onto the fairway where Victoria and Troy had been playing that morning. The golfers would have been appalled to see it now – the parched grass worn bare by the tyres of heavy vehicles and streaked with soot. The woodland had burned down to a no-man's-land of blackened stumps.

A soldier beckoned them into a space between two other trucks, as if he was guiding a plane into a terminal building slot. Petra heaved on the wheel, manoeuvred the engine into the space and stopped.

A soldier opened the door. 'We'll re-equip your vehicle while you get some rest. Fifteen minutes and you're out again. Leave the keys in the ignition in case we need to move it.'

Wanasri followed Darren out, moving across the seat in slow motion. She had never felt so tired in her life. Her muscles were aching from moving about in the heavy turnout gear, and mentally, too, she felt exhausted. She was grateful to be off duty, but daunted by the thought that she had to be back on in fifteen minutes.

Andy prodded her. 'Come on, lazybones. There's a bottle of iced water with my name on it and you're in my way.'

Darren put out his arms. He lifted her out as if she was a feather and set her down on the ground. 'Come on, let's perk you up.' He knew how she felt. They'd all been rookies once.

Wanasri's feet protested as soon as she started to walk. Her boots were stiff and new and she had been running about in them for so long that her feet were a mass of blisters. Her turnout gear still felt as stiff as a suit of armour. She longed to take it off so that she could move freely. Her head throbbed – probably from dehydration after spending so long in such fierce heat, breathing in hot gases. She wanted to take her helmet off but the peak shielded her eyes from the fierce afternoon sun.

Darren marched her through a row of parked engines to a big khaki tent. Water bottles were stacked in crates along a trestle table. Petra cracked one open and downed the whole lot in one go. Darren thrust one into Wanasri's hands. She twisted the lid off with her teeth, spat the cap out and drank gratefully. The water was warm, but she didn't care. She just needed to sluice away the taste of cinders. The first bottle finished, she scrunched it between her hands and started on a second. Beside her, Petra, Darren and Andy were also gulping away.

It was only when Wanasri was on her third bottle that she was able to take it more slowly and look around. The tent looked incongruous in the middle of all these fire engines, like something from a genteel summer fete. The whole place stank of smoke. Firefighters walked around, massive as grizzly bears in their protective clothes. Everywhere she looked, reflective yellow stripes glinted in the sun. Wisps of steam rose off the engines and everything was coated in oily smoke. She tried not to think how much of that oily residue was from vaporized human remains.

Petra crumpled another finished water bottle and dropped it into an overflowing bin. 'Come on, guys,' she said. 'We'd better make way for others.'

Wanasri, Darren and Andy followed her to the next tent. It looked like a jumble sale, with boxes of equipment laid out on tables. Petra went in, took her radio off her jacket, prised the cover off the battery compartment and swapped her old batteries for fresh ones. Meanwhile a soldier with a clipboard came up to her with her instructions. Petra listened carefully, then returned to the others.

Darren gave Wanasri a pat on the arm. 'Come on, time to get back to work.'

Wanasri couldn't believe their fifteen-minute break had passed so quickly. She followed Darren and Andy back to the truck.

The soldiers were just finishing up. Two of them clipped the pike poles back on the side of the engine. Another rolled up a hose attached to a big water tank.

Petra got in the cab and started the engine as Darren, Andy and Wanasri climbed in the other side.

A soldier stood in front of the truck, beckoning Petra on. She put her hand out of the window and acknowledged him, then eased out towards the perimeter.

As they drove towards the exit, tongues of orange flame continued to flicker among the blackened stumps of trees. The fire was still stalking the camp, trying to get a hold. Once again, soldiers pursued it and smothered it, keeping the firefighters' haven safe.

Petra took Engine 33 back onto the road, out into the fiery city again. Away from the bustle of the camp, they could hear the sounds of the sirens again. The sky glowered black with smoke, the sun blazing through it like a furnace.

Petra changed up to third gear and accelerated towards the town centre, her jaw grimly set. 'We've got new instructions. We're going for a big strategic push. The army are helping too. The teams on the outside are going to drive the fire inwards; the teams on the inside – that includes us – are going to drive it outwards. Hopefully we'll meet in the middle. This is no longer about saving individual structures. It's about putting this fire out once and for all.'

Chapter Seventeen

Ben picked up the jerry can, ducked under the wing of the microlight and unscrewed the big cap on the tank behind the cockpit. Kelly twisted round in her seat to watch him as he refilled the fuel tank. Her hands were encased in white mittens, and as Ben poured the fuel mixture in, she made little twitches, mimicking his movements. Ben got the distinct impression she would rather be doing the job herself.

'When you mixed it,' she said, 'did you use a filter?'

The microlight ran on a mixture of two-stroke oil and lead-free petrol.

'Yes,' said Ben. 'Just like you said.'

'Good. You don't want dirt in the fuel tank or we might stall.'

Once the tank was full Ben stowed the jerry can on its hooks beside the petrol tank.

Kelly had some more orders for him. 'Check the engine is securely bolted to the wing.'

Ben looked at her as though she was crazy. 'Why? I haven't touched it.'

'You always have to check the engine mounts before you take off.'

Ben reached up to the wing, put his hands on either side of the engine and gave it a good shake. 'Is that secure enough?'

'Yes, now check the propeller. If it's got any chips or nicks, it might snap off.'

Ben ran his hands along first one blade, then turned the propeller and did the same with the other. 'Smooth as a baby's bottom.'

Kelly looked affronted. 'A what?'

'As a toddler's ass, I guess you'd say in America,' said Ben, hiding a smile.

Next she made him check the wires that held the wings and the connections to the ailerons, the rudder and the brakes. All of this was standard procedure before take-off.

Finally Kelly was satisfied. 'Let's eat and then we can get going.'

Ben scrubbed his hands with wet wipes, then picked up the bag of sandwiches from the floor and offered it to Kelly.

She stayed where she was, sitting back in the seat, the map on her lap. 'You'll have to feed me.'

Ben laughed, thinking she was joking. 'You're not serious, right?'

Two bandaged hands waved in front of his face. 'If I do it myself I'm gonna make a big mess.'

Ben fished out one of the sandwiches and looked at her dubiously.

Kelly sighed. 'Ben, I'm starving. Just hold the darn thing up and let me take a bite.'

She really wasn't joking. Ben tore the wrapper off and looked around warily. If anyone saw him doing this, he'd die of embarrassment. A big tow-truck was parked at the garage but the driver was occupied filling up with petrol. There was a building site a short distance away but no one there would be able to see them. He held the sandwich out. 'Go on then.'

Kelly took a bite, sat back and chewed thoughtfully. 'This town is weird.'

'Apart from being underground, you mean?'

'Did you see all those ill people in the hospital? This is one unhealthy place.'

'Yeah,' said Ben, his mouth full. He realized Kelly was waiting for another bite and thrust her sandwich towards her mouth.

Kelly bit, chewed and swallowed. 'It must do odd things to people, living underground like that. I mean, look at that building site. When they want a house they don't put up blocks and mortar, they go burrowing.'

Now that she pointed it out, Ben noticed how weird the building site was. A machine like a stubby rocket was boring a tunnel into the ground, disgorging rocks and red sand up a conveyor belt. But he would rather leave the sightseeing until they'd got the embarrassing business of feeding Kelly out of the way. He held up the sandwich. 'Eat.'

She opened her mouth.

Instead of taking a bite, she jumped, nearly

knocking the sandwich out of Ben's hand. 'What the hell—?'

A dark figure was standing just outside, staring in at them: an Aboriginal child of about seven. He had dark brown skin and thick wavy hair.

Two more children appeared beside him – another Aboriginal, with a red plaited cord around his neck, and a younger blonde girl.

Ben wanted the ground to open up and swallow him. If one of his mates in Macclesfield had found him feeding sandwiches to a girl, his life wouldn't have been worth living.

But Kelly had no thought for his blushes. She recovered from her fright and took another big bite of the sandwich. 'Run along and play,' she said to the children, her mouth full.

Three pairs of eyes watched them in astonishment.

Kelly took the last piece of sandwich and Ben decided to try to explain. 'She's hurt herself,' he said, hoping that would make him look a bit less soppy.

That wasn't what the children were interested in. The Aboriginal with the red cord reached out a hand and stroked the microlight's wing. The other one also put his hand on the plane. 'Did you come here in this?' he asked.

'Yes,' said Kelly. 'Now beat it.'

She still had her mouth full but Ben couldn't mistake the irritation stirring in her voice. He guessed she didn't relish chatting to seven-year-olds.

The blonde girl reached a grubby finger towards Kelly's bandages. 'Have your hands been cut off?'

'Go away,' said Kelly. 'We're going to start the engine in a minute. The propeller will cut *your* hands off if you stand too close.'

The girl looked as though she might do as she was told, but the two older children didn't want to leave the microlight. The first child turned to the other one and asked him, 'Is this like the real big bird that disappears?'

'No, that was bigger. This one looks like a kind of bike.'

Kelly glared at them. Ben scrunched up the sandwich wrappers and smirked.

'What's the bird that disappears?' asked the little girl.

'You're too young to know about that,' her companion with the red cord told her.

'They might have seen it,' said red necklace. He turned to Kelly. 'Have you?'

'No, I haven't,' snapped Kelly.

'Describe it to her,' said the other Aborigine.

Red necklace leaned into the cockpit. 'I'll have to whisper.'

Kelly glanced at Ben, hoping for rescue, but she was cornered in her seat. Like it or not, she was going to be told. The child leaned close and whispered in her ear. When he had finished, he straightened up and looked at her solemnly, waiting for her response.

Kelly shook her head. 'No, I haven't seen any UFOs. Now buzz off. I mean it. We're going to start the engine and it's extremely dangerous for you to be this close to the plane.'

A woman appeared at the door of the petrol station and beckoned to them. The children turned round and ran across with a flat-footed gait that kicked up clouds of red dust. They weren't wearing any shoes.

Kelly didn't waste any time. 'Start the darn engine, before they come back.'

Ben turned the key. The engine spluttered, then settled to a low purr, with the propeller turning slowly. An enormous grin spread over his face. He was going to take off.

'Don't get too excited,' said Kelly. 'We're not going anywhere yet. We have to run the engine for five minutes to get it up to operating temperature.' She sat back and shook her head. 'This place is the Midwest Down Under.'

'What did that kid tell you?' said Ben.

'Some nonsense. His uncle went walkabout in the bush at night and saw lights in the sky.'

'Is that the big bird that disappears?' asked Ben.

'Don't be stupid.' Kelly brushed crumbs off the map with her forearms. She put on a high, squeaky voice. '*A big bird came down, and when it landed, it disappeared.*' She reverted to her normal voice. 'That's how six-year-olds talk about UFOs.'

'No they don't,' said Ben. 'They talk about spacemen. Big birds that vanish sounds like a dreamtime story.'

Kelly checked the temperature gauge. 'You can skip the culture lesson. We're ready to go.'

They did a few final checks. Under Kelly's direction, Ben set the trim – rebalancing the craft to adjust for the weight of the fuel they had added. He secured the doors and fastened the seat belts, reaching around Kelly's waist to do up hers.

'Thirteen and never been kissed?' said Kelly.

He felt himself blush as he fumbled with the seat belt catch. Finally it locked. 'There!' he said in relief.

'OK.' Kelly's tone was brisk now. 'Start by pointing the nose down.'

Ben looked at the controls in front of him. His mind had gone blank again. He couldn't remember how to point the nose down.

'With the stick!' exclaimed Kelly. 'For heaven's sake. I should have got one of those kids as my co-pilot.'

If Ben had felt more relaxed, he might have reminded her that one of them thought the microlight looked like a bike. As it was, he was too pre-occupied struggling to remember what instrument did what. He moved the stick forward as far as it would go.

'While you're sitting there like a dork, I'm thinking about our take-off. We've got a clear run along this road here. Windspeed and direction are fine – let's have the throttle fully open and off we go.'

Ben pulled the throttle up. The propeller became a blur, the engine let out a roar and the rev counter climbed sharply. But they didn't move.

Kelly batted her hand towards the stick. 'Take the handbrake off!'

Ben winced and slipped the piece of Velcro off the handle.

Released from its fetters, the microlight shot forwards.

Ben had forgotten how rickety it felt. The cables through the cockpit twanged like guitar strings, the wheels rattled, and the steering seemed to have a mind of its own.

'We're veering left,' snapped Kelly. 'Keep straight with your pedals and the stick. Use the horizon.'

Ben nudged the pedals and stick until they were heading dead straight down the road. He had a sudden vision of meeting a juggernaut or a coachload of tourists head on.

The stick kept twitching in his hand, as though the nose was trying to come up. 'It feels like it wants to fly,' he said. He felt quite proud that he'd noticed that.

'You're not going fast enough yet – if you haven't

got enough speed you'll stall. Just keep going like this.'

Ben glanced at the airspeed. It said 40 knots. With all this twanging and rattling it seemed like 140. He felt particularly reckless to be doing this on a public road. If this was England, by now he would have met the juggernaut and the tourist coach, plus several dozen parents doing the school run. The speed crept up to 50 knots . . . 51, 52 . . .

'Ease the nose up,' said Kelly, 'and keep her level.'

At last. Butterflies were dancing a fandango in Ben's stomach. He eased the stick back, keeping his eyes firmly on the horizon. The slightest deviation in straightness and he would be ready to make a correction.

As the wheels left the ground, the rattling disappeared and the ride became smooth as silk. The horizon slipped away. The plane soared into the air.

'Keep this speed,' said Kelly, 'and climb to a thousand feet.' Already she was looking down at the map on her knee. 'But well done. That was pretty good.'

Ben felt a warm glow spread through him. He'd

actually got a plane into the air all on his own. A little voice in his mind was saying 'Wow', over and over again.

But Kelly wasn't about to let him rest on his laurels. 'Keep straight.'

Ben started to correct when suddenly he looked down at the pedals.

Something was moving in the foot well. Something like a grey hand.

'Don't look down there,' scolded Kelly. 'You're meant to be climbing. You can't relax yet – this is a critical stage.'

Ben looked ahead and tweaked the nose up, just to make sure. Then, once again, he felt something tickle his leg. He looked down—

His leg jerked violently before he'd even got the scream out. The microlight wobbled and the wings tilted. Ben's shoulder hit his door with a thump.

Kelly tried to hold onto the seat. She pumped the pedals to bring them straight and yelled, 'Have you gone nuts?'

'There's a spider as big as my hand!' Ben couldn't

look anywhere but the foot well. The spider was big and furry, with long, long legs.

'Oh, grow up. This isn't some Indiana Jones movie.' Kelly tried to straighten the plane up but her bandaged hand pulled the stick too far. The microlight rolled violently the other way. She pushed the stick and stamped hard with the pedal to stop them going right over, then lifted her foot to release it.

At that moment the spider crawled onto Ben's boot. He tried to shake it off and his foot shot forward. On the other side, Kelly pressed down on her pedal, making Ben's snap down on his foot, pinning it.

She screamed in fury. 'Get your foot out of the way!'

With his foot imprisoned, the spider got a good purchase and started to climb up his leg. Ben jerked his feet away from the pedals but that didn't dislodge it.

The microlight rolled from one side to another. 'We're losing airspeed!' Kelly tried to pull the throttle up with her elbow, then turned and took the stick crudely between her wrists. To do so, she had to twist round in her seat, and found herself staring straight at Ben's thigh.

The spider had a big brown furry body like a mouse, black glinting eyes and long spindly legs. A dainty pair of incisors curved downwards like a Victorian moustache. It was barely half a metre away from Kelly's face.

Despite herself, Kelly recoiled in horror, jerking the stick and making the microlight dive once again. She shrank back against her door and shifted the stick back again with her elbow. 'More throttle, quick!'

Ben increased the throttle, never taking his eyes from the spider. It felt heavy as it walked further up his leg, and he felt every movement of its eight legs through the thin fabric of his flying suit.

Kelly screamed hysterically, shadow-boxing the air with her bandaged paws. 'Get it out! Just get it out!'

'How?' Ben shouted, equally hysterical. He jerked his leg, hoping to shake the spider loose, but it wouldn't shift. Did it have suckers on its legs?

'Just do something!'

Careful to keep his body absolutely still, Ben put his hand out of the window. The catch on the door was fiddly but he managed to open it. The door swung back and smacked against the nose of the plane. The red ground yawned outside.

Kelly's voice shrieked in his headset. 'Are you nuts?'

Ben jerked his leg towards the open door but the spider remained stuck fast. If he touched it there was the risk that it might bite him. 'Get off me, you ugly devil,' he told it through clenched teeth.

Kelly's hand waved in his face as she adjusted the stick with her left elbow.

Ben grabbed her arm and used her bandaged hand to bat the spider away. If it attacked, he figured its fangs weren't long enough to bite through all the bandages. Kelly screamed and the spider flew out of the door, became a black blob in the bright sunshine and vanished to a pinpoint.

'Happy landings,' said Ben with feeling.

He let go of Kelly's hand and reached to pull the door shut. It had swung right open and was flapping to and fro. He had to brace his hand on the door frame and lean out. His fingers caught the door, got a purchase and pulled it shut.

He sat back, catching his breath.

Kelly's voice came through on the headset, hoarse

and strained. 'Do you mind sorting out this plane before we crash?'

As Ben took the controls, he saw that the ground looked alarmingly close: sure enough, when he checked the instruments, he found they were at 360 feet. He nudged the stick forward and swooped down a little way to get a good burst of speed, then opened the throttle and soared upwards. He watched the altimeter, kept the craft straight, and made sure they were cruising to textbook standards before relaxing and turning to Kelly.

She was sitting back in her seat and cradling her hand.

Ben winced. 'Did I hurt you?'

'No, I don't think so. Those painkillers must be pretty good.'

But while Kelly didn't mind Ben grabbing her arm too much, she did have a few other things to get off her chest. She sat up straight and fixed him with a furious glare. 'The next time something like that happens, don't panic like that. You do not ever start jerking your feet around in a light aeroplane. I thought you were having an epileptic fit!'

Ben was stunned. Now she was blaming him? 'Whereas you were a picture of self-control, I suppose?' he muttered resentfully.

Kelly didn't seem to hear him. She had more to say; plenty more. 'We nearly rolled over – if you do that in a microlight, you'll snap the wing off. We were flying dangerously low and the speed we were going we could easily have crashed. That was a very immature way to react – and by the way, you never, ever, ever – under any circumstances – *open the door.*'

She gestured towards the door and nearly biffed him on the nose with her pristine white bandage – now marked with a big yellowy smudge.

'You've – er – got a bit of something on your bandage. I think it's spider entrails,' Ben told her.

Bel walked along a shopping street. The windows were grimy and dark. In a clothes shop, a dummy lay across the doorway. Its hair and face had melted. At first Bel thought its body had been painted green, then realized that the clothes it was wearing had melted too.

Had she seen this dummy before? she wondered.

Was this the shop near the green where she'd fallen over among all those insects? Was she going around in circles? She felt so disorientated. Wisps of smoke and steam rose from the ruined shops, as though the fires inside were not truly vanquished but sleeping, like dormant volcanoes.

The asphalt under her feet had softened in the heat. The heavy fire engine wheels had pushed it up to the edges of the kerb so that it looked like a fallen soufflé.

She was no longer wet. The heat radiating from the scorched streets had dried her clothes in no time. They felt stiff with sweat and dirt, as though they had been starched. There hardly seemed to be anyone else about. Had they all been picked up in rescue vehicles?

Approaching a junction, she noticed a burned-out car that had rammed into a lamppost. There was nothing left of its interior: the seats and controls were vaporized, leaving only bare metal – though its back window remained intact; it was covered in stickers. Although they were blackened, the lettering showed in a different texture so they were still readable. Bel recognized them because they were from environ-mental campaigns she had played a part in: NUCLEAR

POWER, NO THANKS. AGAINST GLOBAL WARMING. The car had belonged to people like her. Maybe she even knew them. There was another sticker, less familiar to her. She looked closer and tried to trace the lettering: OZ PROTECTORS FOR A HEALTHY PLANET.

If the car had had any tyres left she would have kicked them. These were the people who had kidnapped Major Kurtis, locked her up and left her to burn. Now their car was wrecked. Well, that was poetic justice.

But then a cold feeling stole over her. The car had crashed into that lamppost. She imagined the scene: had the petrol tank gone up and consumed the occupants in flames? Had Major Kurtis been in the car too?

What a horrible way to die, to burn to death in a car. She felt sick to her stomach. She'd wanted revenge, but in some civilized way; she'd wanted them to face justice.

No, they must have got out, she decided. If they hadn't, there would still be some human remains, surely. And the car might not belong to the same people who grabbed her. Any environmentally aware person might display stickers like that. Still, if she ever crossed paths with Oz Protectors again . . .

She did not know that she already had; that they had suffered only a slightly less dreadful fate, choking to death on the chemical fumes in the swimming baths.

Down a street to the left she saw a group of fire-fighters and an engine. Thank God! At last – people. She ran towards them.

They were working on the cinema. The three-storey frontage had collapsed, along with the ground floor, and blackened concrete beams spanned a big hole into the basement. Three firefighters were directing their hoses down into it. But the water wasn't blasting out at high pressure; it was trickling out gently, as if they were cleaning something fragile. There was something very eerie about the whole scene.

Bel found her eye drawn into the hole. She saw shapes below the section of wall, a jumble of light and dark, slick with water. It reminded her of a shoreline after an oil disaster. Everything looked different after a fire had done its work. Was that a metal chair? A café table? The more she looked, the more she recognized. Water was trickling down from the hoses above, washing away some of the soot so that the bright metal of the tables and chairs showed through.

The trickling water revealed something else as well. Pale rods protruded out of the black slick. They were bones from toes. A human foot.

Before she could look away her brain made sense of more shadows – part of a leg.

'Ma'am.' Bel suddenly noticed a firefighter standing in front of her. A girl. Her face seemed familiar – the oriental features smeared with black stripes, the firefighting clothes bulking out her rangy frame, making her look like an American footballer. Had she spoken to her earlier that day? Or maybe it was shock that made her imagine that.

She pointed into the basement. 'There's somebody down there.' Her voice came out in a whisper – she felt terribly shaken. She had often seen dead bodies when she visited disaster zones but it was something you never got used to; particularly when they had been burned.

Even as she said it, she realized the firefighters must already know the body was there. That's why their hoses weren't on full blast.

'Ma'am,' said the firefighter, 'you can't stay here. You must move on.'

Bel looked into the firefighter's face and saw weariness. She was just a kid. She could only be a few years older than Ben. What terrible things must she have seen today? And yet she was being so calm. Disasters made people grow up so quickly. Bel felt ashamed of her own moment of weakness. She made an effort to pull herself together. She let the firefighter escort her away from the yawning pit and towards the truck. Hose lines snaked out of the back, throbbing with the water that was travelling down them. The sound of it pulsing towards the wreckage drew Bel's gaze back there again.

She saw a tongue of flame flickering up the side of the building. The firefighters responded immediately: suddenly the water came out in a strong white jet and they lashed the walls. In less than a minute the flames were beaten back to smoke.

Then they reduced the flow to a gentle trickle once more and turned back to their patient work down in the basement.

'Is there somewhere safe where I can go?' said Bel.

Wanasri took her to the fire truck and opened a hatch in its metal side. She brought out the spare fire jacket and put it around Bel's shoulders, then went back and fetched a bottle of water.

'Wait here and you can ride back to the station with us,' she said. 'But it looks as though we'll be here for hours yet.'

Bel felt the weight of the jacket and slipped her arms into the sleeves. She wanted to say thanks, but tears of relief welled up in her throat instead. She nodded and sat down against the chrome bumper of the engine. Wanasri hurried back to rejoin her colleagues.

Engine 33's crew were working on the cinema as a break from active firefighting. The teams could only work in flames and smoke for so long, so they had been sent to work at a low-risk site – a job that was actually no less harrowing than fighting fires. They were recovering badly burned bodies.

Petra, Andy and Darren were gently hosing the bodies down to cool them off – stopping them from burning and deteriorating further, which would make identification impossible. Wanasri's job was to prevent the public seeing the bodies.

They decided they needed to move a section of debris and Wanasri went back to the engine to fetch some lifting equipment.

The woman she had left sitting against the fender was on her feet.

'Are you feeling better?' asked Wanasri.

Bel fastened the jacket briskly. 'I feel fine now, so I'll be off,' she said. 'There are some trucks down at the end of that road – I'll go down there and hitch a ride. It's better than sitting here for hours – I'll get in your way, and anyhow, I'll go mad if I just sit here. Thanks again for your help.'

'Are you sure?' said Wanasri.

But Bel was already marching away, her arms swinging determinedly.

Chapter Eighteen

While Ben flew, Kelly pored over the map. She had taken a reading off the GPS – the global positioning system – and was lining it up with the grid reference on the map. Her big paw-bandages traced the grid lines.

While trying to get rid of the spider, neither of them had noticed the plane's bearing. They had gone way off course.

When she found the reference, she wasn't exactly pleased. 'We are literally in the middle of nowhere,' she said. 'This place is just empty. It just says "Great Victoria Desert" on the map and there's nothing else at all. No roads, no water features, nothing.'

Ben had done a bit of orienteering. 'What about lining up on contour lines?'

Kelly waved a white fist in the direction of the window. 'Do you see any hills? There are no hills so there are no contour lines. We are in the middle of a big empty space.'

'Could be why they call it the outback,' said Ben. 'But we don't need the map, do we? We've got the GPS.'

'The GPS could go wrong or it could run out of battery power. You should always use a map too. I really don't like it when I can't see where I am on paper.'

Ben got the feeling that the real reason she was fretting so much was that she was worried about her father.

'I'm trying to find the Ghan track,' said Kelly after a while.

'But the police stopped the Ghan. They weren't on board.'

'My dad wouldn't make a mistake,' said Kelly. 'The kidnappers must have taken them off the train before the police searched it.'

'If they were ever on it in the first place.'

Kelly sat in silence for a few moments. 'They had to be,' she said at last. 'Otherwise they'd still be back in Adelaide. And the doctor at Coober Pedy told me that Adelaide's on fire.'

'What do you mean, Adelaide's on fire?'

'The whole town,' said Kelly. 'They think it spread down from the vineyards.'

'The vineyards?' repeated Ben. 'But that was hours ago! It can't still be burning. Why didn't you tell me before? What if my mum's still there?'

Kelly glared at him. 'Listen, don't start getting snippy with me. All I know is that it's a big emergency. And there's nobody there because the army is evacuating the place. Just chill.'

Ben seethed. He had just as much right to worry about his mum as she had to worry about her father. But he decided to keep his feelings to himself. Another argument wouldn't help them.

'We need to follow the track back to Adelaide,' he said. 'Maybe if they were taken off we'll see some sign.'

'They're a couple of tiny needles in one mother

of a big haystack . . .' mused Kelly, looking down.

Certainly the terrain below was bleak – mile upon mile of featureless red earth like the surface of Mars. At least it should be straightforward to fly over, with no thermals from hills and valleys. All the same, Ben would have been glad to see a hill. All this Martian flatness was a bit unsettling. Nothing changed. It was as if they were hanging stationary in mid air.

Kelly looked at the instruments and tutted. 'You're taking us in the wrong direction. Turn in a big circle.'

Ben eased the stick over.

Kelly gave a weary sigh and looked down at the map again. 'We're never going to get back to Adelaide if you let us drift off course like this.'

Ben wasn't finding turning as easy as he'd expected. The rudder didn't want to work – yet the microlight was normally so responsive. Now it was like trying to steer a supermarket trolley.

'Kelly,' he said, 'try your left rudder.'

He felt her press the pedal. That did nothing either.

'It's the wind,' she said. 'We're in a really strong gale. More throttle!'

Ben increased the throttle. The engine noise grew

higher and faster and he expected the airspeed indicator to climb quite quickly, but it hardly moved. 'Nose down?' he asked Kelly.

She nodded. 'Absolutely.'

Ben eased the nose down, hoping a shallow dive would give them extra speed. The red dusty landscape filled his windscreen. Normally, if you were flying in a strong wind you could see its effects, but because there were no trees everything looked eerily still. The only sign was the red horizon blurring into the cobalt sky, as though it was being brushed vigorously.

Ben's manoeuvre worked and the craft picked up a little speed. But as soon as he eased off the throttle or let the nose level out, they slowed right down, almost to stall speed.

'That is some strong wind,' said Kelly. 'We are going to burn up a lot of fuel—'

Her words ended in a scream that made Ben jump in his seat.

'Arghh! Get it off me!' She looked down at her flying suit and scrubbed at her legs with her bandage-mittened hands. 'Get it off!' She jerked her leg like Ben had when he was trying to get rid of the spider.

Ben pointed the nose down into another shallow dive. The plane would keep that course on its own for a few seconds while he tried to help Kelly. She was wriggling frantically, jerking both legs up and down. But as far as Ben could see, there was nothing on her.

'Kelly, I can't see it – what is it? Another spider?'

She rubbed her hands furiously along her legs, as if trying to brush something away. 'Get it off! Get it off me!' She was becoming hysterical.

Ben still couldn't see anything. He looked up and down her legs and in the foot well, expecting another set of spidery legs or some other creepy crawly. He remembered the leaflet he'd read in the hotel, which listed a whole army of deadly nasties. What else had got in with that spider? Had it bitten her?

Kelly shuddered. The movement went through her whole body. 'They're all over me,' she said in a high, panicky voice. She was battering at her flying suit with her mittened hands, heedless of the pain. Her feet thundered on the pedals and the microlight shook from side to side.

Ben leaned over. He couldn't see anything – either on her or in the foot well – although it was difficult to know for sure because she would not keep still.

Kelly looked at him with wild eyes. 'Do something! They're crawling all over me!' She shook violently again, but this time, mercifully, with her feet away from the pedals. Her blonde hair came free of her baseball cap.

Ben made a decision. He couldn't continue flying with her in that state. He would have to find some-where to land.

He looked out of the window and got a surprise. They must have gone quite a distance because instead of featureless red terrain he saw a cluster of isolated buildings and a huge white dome.

He'd aim for that. It was his best hope of getting help.

Beside him, Kelly shuddered and batted the air. Maybe she was having some kind of fit. Or maybe something had bitten her and she was reacting to poison.

'Kelly,' said Ben, 'I'm going to land. Talk me through it.'

Kelly was trying to scratch herself but the bandages stopped her. 'Just get us down!' she managed to say.

Ben felt a trickle of cold sweat down the back of his neck. She wasn't going to be any help. He would have to take the plane down on his own.

He tried to remember what they'd done before. He had to find a long, straight stretch of clear ground to use as a runway – well, that shouldn't be a problem. He brought the plane down to 500 feet and studied the layout. A high steel mesh fence enclosed an area of several acres. As well as several long single-storey sheds there was a large white dome. The ground between the buildings was striped with vehicle tracks. He wondered if it might be some kind of power station. But why out here in the desert, a thousand kilometres from civilization?

At one end was a clear stretch of land with no buildings on it, only a fence. There were no rocks strewn across it either – that was a bonus. It seemed tailor-made for landing a plane. There was also a bright orange windsock fluttering gently against a flagpole. Well, you couldn't get more handy than that. Except . . . he couldn't remember. Was he meant to land into the wind or against it?

And now he thought about it, where had that

strong wind disappeared to? The microlight was steering easily again. The orange windsock down below was hardly stirring.

Kelly gave another scream and squirmed in the seat. She put her wrist up to her mouth and tried to tear at the bandages with her teeth. Ben put his hand out and pushed her hand away, stopping her.

She rewarded him with a snarl. 'I need to scratch!'

He had to let go of her wrist. He needed both hands on the controls. Especially as he was now at 300 feet. 'Fine,' he snapped back. 'Don't blame me if the burns go septic then.'

Kelly bit the bandage and pulled.

Outside the window, the features on the ground were getting bigger. Before, Kelly had made him fly circles over his intended landing site to check it out. There was no time for that now.

The plane started to wobble as it encountered air currents stirred up from the ground. Ben worked the pedals and stick to keep it level. I can do this, he thought. Easy peasy.

He looked at his airspeed. Still 70 knots –

cruising speed. They needed to be going slower. He'd forgotten about that. He pushed the throttle right down.

The revs needle dropped and above his head the engine fell suddenly silent. He'd closed it down too far. The plane had stalled!

He opened the throttle a little more, his heart in his mouth. Fortunately the engine restarted, its beat steady and true.

He was lined up on his runway now. The ground was a lot closer. He could see pebbles like the grain in an old photo when you enlarged it.

Suddenly the plane lurched. The altimeter dropped to 20 feet. Then it swung the other way to 2000. The airspeed needle beat from side to side like a wind-screen wiper. The GPS screen went blank, then flashed up a message in block capitals: ERROR.

'That doesn't happen in Microsoft Flight Simulator,' thought Ben.

He tapped the dials, then looked at Kelly, hoping for help. She was unravelling her right bandage, twitching her shoulders up and down to try to scratch them on the inside of her jumpsuit.

His instruments were going haywire. Now how would he get down safely?

Outside, the ground was very close. The vehicle tracks had become distinct tyre marks and were getting further and further apart. He tried to guess how far he had to go but his unpractised eye hadn't a clue. He'd just have to guess.

He put the throttle right down and eased the nose up.

It suddenly occurred to him that if the instruments were out, the controls might not work either.

The front wheel bumped on the ground, then the back wheels followed it with a thump. Not the right way to get down, but at least they were on the ground. The only problem now was stopping.

The engine stalled again. He'd landed closer to the end fence than he intended and was freewheeling towards it at high speed.

He squeezed on the brakes hard. The nose slewed round and his view of the fence disappeared in a cloud of red dust.

He only hoped the brakes would pull them up before they slammed into the fence.

Something prodded his chest so hard it made him jump in his seat. It was like the kick of an electric shock. He took his left hand off the throttle and brushed it away, but the sensation seemed to jump to his leg. He jerked his leg and the plane swung around as his foot caught the pedal. Something ran up his spine – something that felt like it had a lot of legs. He forgot about the brake and the pedals, let go of the stick and tried to undo his seat belt so that he could get this creature off him. Another one ran across his shoulder. Then they started coming up his thighs and arms. He tried to get them off, his hands flailing against the roof of the cockpit and the window.

Gradually the awful crawling sensation stopped. He realized the plane had stopped too. Kelly had her bandaged hands around the brake like pincers. Cautiously she let go and sat up slowly. One bandage was trailing from her right hand. Outside the windscreen the dust was settling. They had stopped just metres from the steel mesh fence. At a speed similar to fifty miles an hour it would have sliced them like cheese in a grater.

Kelly let out a long breath. 'You felt it too?'

She seemed to be normal again.

Ben was still getting his breath back. 'Yeah. What was it?'

'I don't know,' said Kelly. 'I thought it was insects or something at first. But it was more like an electric shock.'

Ben nodded. 'Maybe there's some exposed wiring.'

Kelly put her arm up to wipe the sweat away from her forehead and looked at the trailing bandage in surprise. She held it out to Ben. 'I don't think I should have done this.'

She hadn't actually managed to get much of it off. While Ben tied it up around her wrist she looked over the back of the seat. 'I wonder where we are . . . Uh-oh.' She went tense.

Ben turned in the seat and looked behind them. The dust was blowing up again. Was it a dust storm?

Then they saw a big bright light looming out of the sky like a spotlight, and heard the noise. The entire sky was roaring. The light was getting lower and closer. What was it?

Next they made out the high whine of jet engines.

A big shadow like an arrowhead began to take shape in the swirling dust.

'That's a plane,' said Kelly. 'A very big plane. And we're on the end of its runway.'

Ben turned the ignition key. The engine coughed and spluttered but wouldn't turn over.

Kelly waved her paw at him. 'There must be dust in the filter. Quick, get out!'

Ben snapped the door catch up and jumped out of the microlight. He ran round to Kelly's side, noticing as he did so that the plane was looming bigger in the sky, its engine noise deafening. He released the catch on her door and she tumbled out and started running. They sprinted along the fence, away from the approaching monster.

The light was under the plane's belly. It illuminated a vast grey fuselage and a big row of wheels. The back wheels touched down and Ben felt the impact reverberate through his bones. The nose came down, obscuring the light on the belly of the craft. A wave of sand blasted towards him and Kelly. They shrank back against the fence, shielding their eyes with their hands. The engines screamed in their ears as the pilot put the brakes on.

The engine whine diminished. When they opened their eyes, the plane had slowed right down to a sedate taxiing speed. The clouds of dust were settling around it.

The plane came towards them and then turned. Ben and Kelly gasped.

It was massive – almost as long as a football field and as high as a six-storey building; big and grey with a rounded nose. The wheeled undercarriage alone was huge – a mass of wheels and struts.

Kelly was transfixed by the plane. 'Unless I'm very much mistaken,' she said, 'that is a Galaxy Starlifter. It can take off and land on a dime. It doesn't need a runway or air traffic control because it's got all the weather radar on board. It can fit six entire Greyhound buses in its hold.' She was back in teacher mode.

'Delivering buses by plane?' said Ben. 'Isn't that like buying a dog and barking yourself?'

'I thought you'd be impressed. That's one of the world's largest aircraft. It travels as fast as a jet plane. Don't boys like things like that?'

Ben was definitely impressed – it was just more fun not to show it.

The plane was heading for the open doors of a giant hangar. At the front end, the nose sprang open and folded back over the cockpit. It looked like someone had cut the nose off a shark and hinged it upwards. The dust settled a little more, enough for them to see there was lettering on the plane's tail: USAF – United States Air Force. Then the doors closed. All that remained of the plane was the red dust blowing over its massive wheel-ruts.

'There's your real big bird that disappears,' mused Ben.

Kelly stood up straight. 'We're on home turf,' she said. 'These guys are Americans. I think we'd better go and say hello.'

'It's *your* home turf,' grumbled Ben as he set off behind her. 'You Americans – you think you own the world.'

In the distance, a figure was standing outside one of the huts. He wore a military-looking uniform of faded blue. He seemed to be on a smoking break. He threw a cigarette butt down onto the ground and stubbed it out with his foot. Then he opened the door and went back inside.

Kelly looked around. The microlight was close to the perimeter fence, in the shadow of the gigantic dome. 'I think we can leave our little buzzmobile here. It's not in anybody's way. Come on.' She pushed her headset down around her neck like a torque and set off in the direction of the door, bandaged hands swinging purposefully. She looked a peculiar figure: her flying suit grimy with desert dust, open to the navel to reveal her orange T-shirt, headset discarded around her neck, bandaged hands like two white mittens. Ben looked down at his own flying suit. It was none too clean either. He tried to brush the worst of it off as he walked. Somehow he thought it might not make a good impression to look as if he'd just climbed out of a dumper truck.

It took them a good five minutes just to walk past the dome. It was massive: at least 80 feet tall – only half as tall as the Millennium Dome, but then that wasn't out in the middle of the Australian desert. The surface was covered in a thick white plastic material. It looked like a set for a *Star Wars* movie.

Ben's mind was working furiously as he walked along beside Kelly. An American base in the middle of the Australian desert? He felt in his pocket and pulled out the flyer from Oz Protectors:

Not far from Adelaide, in the Great Victoria Desert, the Americans built a listening station. Ever since, the people of Coober Pedy have been stricken by a number of strange sicknesses.

'Kelly,' said Ben, showing her the leaflet, 'do you remember this? This is the place they're talking about.'

'Probably.' Kelly nodded.

'It's the place that's been making everyone sick in Coober Pedy.'

'Oh, that's just anti-American propaganda.'

Ben shrugged. It probably was, but as he tucked the flyer back into his pocket he had a moment of déjà vu: putting the flyer in that same pocket while the café owner in Coober Pedy said, *I had this terrible itching. I thought my skin was crawling with insects . . .*

They reached the door where they had seen the

figure in the blue uniform. Kelly stood aside for Ben to open it.

He still had misgivings. 'Should we really be here?'

Kelly glared at him. 'Why not?'

He looked at that curled lip and the interrogating eyes and couldn't quite think how to begin.

She didn't give him long to explain. 'Oh, don't be a scaredy-cat. I've been on these bases before. My dad's in the army, remember? It'll be fine. Come on, let's go in.'

Inside was a dark corridor and an open door into a lighted room. Kelly led the way.

The room was some kind of laboratory. Ben was reminded of pictures he'd seen of mission control in Houston during the Moon landings. Except that the whole place seemed to be manned by just two people. They were surrounded by so much electronic equipment that it took him a few seconds to spot them. Each man had three computer monitors. Along the walls were metal racks holding more banks of equipment covered with flashing lights. Some of the equipment had a home-made look. The knobs and lights were different sizes, as if they had been fitted at different times. The numbers and lettering on the labels didn't match. It looked like a prototype machine that someone was constantly building and refining; like something out of Ben's dad's workshop in the back garden. Except that everything here was emblazoned with the insignia of the US army.

Both scientists wore the muted blue uniform. They seemed wrapped up in their work and didn't take much notice of the newcomers. Ben's dad was like that when he was concentrating.

'The frequency's stabilized,' said one of the men. A label on his shirt said his name was Grishkevich. He was looking at one of the screens. On it was a satellite picture like the ones on weather programmes. Grishkevich pressed a cursor key. The map view moved down a few centimetres. He looked at it carefully and then at another map picture on another screen, comparing them.

The other scientist, whose name tag said Hijkoop, looked over his shoulder at his screens.

'It doesn't seem to have made any difference,' said Grishkevich. 'The wind's died down to five knots but it could kick up again any minute.'

'Hi,' said Kelly.

Grishkevich continued to ignore her but Hijkoop looked up. 'Ah, you got here at last. Are you guys new? I haven't seen you before.'

Grishkevich spoke too, but he kept his eyes glued to the screen. 'Sorry – you must have had a rough ride on the way in. We're having a lot of trouble with it today.' He continued to move the picture with his cursor.

'They'll have breezed in with no trouble,' said Hijkoop. 'That crate is big enough to cope with a bit of bad weather. You guys must get much worse in Alaska.'

Ben realized the scientists thought they'd come in on the Galaxy Starlifter. Of course, with their flying suits and the headsets around their necks, it was a reasonable assumption to make. Although they obviously couldn't have looked at Kelly properly because she looked more like a teenage tourist than a military scientist. And people always assumed that Ben was older than thirteen, though he was sure he didn't look old enough to be in the army just yet.

Hijkoop chuckled. 'Alaskan winter to Australian

summer. I bet that's a shock. Did you bring us some ice? We haven't managed to make snow yet but we're working on it.'

Grishkevich stood up. He brushed imaginary dust off his trousers. 'OK, show us what you've got for us. I hope it's not Alaska's cast-offs.'

Ben was wondering if they could sneak out quietly before they got into trouble, but Kelly was determined to put them right. 'We didn't fly here from Alaska. We've just come from Adelaide.'

Hijkoop and Grishkevich stopped what they were doing and looked at Ben and Kelly properly for the first time.

Ben saw their expressions change. Hijkoop reached behind his monitor screens and pulled out the plugs. The satellite weather pictures vanished.

Kelly drew herself up to her full height. 'I'm a United States citizen and I need help. My father is an army officer and he's been kidnapped in Adelaide.'

Grishkevich snatched up some files and clutched them to his chest protectively. He glared at Ben and Kelly. His entire manner had suddenly changed and he looked very angry. 'How did you get in here?'

'We got lost,' said Ben. 'There was some bad weather. We got blown off course.'

Hijkoop was on the phone. 'Security, we need help. We've got intruders.' He put the phone down and looked at Ben and Kelly. 'That story isn't going to wash. You don't just wander into a high security base like this. Who are you really? How did you get in?'

'We'll have you in court for trespass,' said Grishkevich. 'They'll lock you up and throw away the key. How many of you are here?'

'It's just us,' said Ben.

Kelly looked offended. 'I'll have you know that my father—'

Suddenly an alarm wailed through the building.

Ben pulled at Kelly's arm and quickly dragged her out of the room.

In the corridor, she pulled out of his grasp, looking outraged. 'I can explain to them.'

Ben took her arm and hissed in her ear. 'You can't. Look.' He opened the cargo pocket on his trousers a little way, just enough to show her the piece of paper in there. STOP SECRET US EXPERIMENTS. He still had the Oz Protectors flyer.

Kelly stared in disbelief. 'You dummy. Why didn't you throw that away before?'

'Well, I didn't think we'd be coming here.'

'If they search you and find that, they'll throw our asses in jail.'

Behind, they heard people running down the corridor. Voices rang out, barking orders: 'Use reasonable force. Shoot to wound, not to kill.'

'Screw that,' yelled Kelly. 'Run!'

Snoopy sat in the back of an army truck with a blanket around his shoulders. 'Look at that, dude,' he said to Dodge. 'Awesome!'

They were watching the flames and smoke that spread from one edge of the skyline to the other. The whole of Adelaide was ablaze.

Dodge was coughing. 'I got a bloody lungful of smoke, Snoop. Should come with a public health warning, eh?' They laughed.

An army medic came over with water bottles for them both. 'You're going to feel weak because of the smoke inhalation,' he said.

'No kidding,' said Dodge. He nodded towards the

burning buildings. 'Do they know how it got started?'

'Some idiot lit a fire, probably,' said the medic.

Snoopy tutted. 'No consideration, some people.'

The medic looked at them with a frown. 'You need to keep your fluid intake up. Drink. Other than that, stay still. We're going to be moving out in a few minutes, as soon as we've picked up a few more survivors.'

Dodge squirted some water over his tongue and grimaced. 'Tell you what, mate,' he said to the medic. 'You wouldn't happen to have a cold beer, would you?'

It wasn't often that the desert base got unwelcome visitors, but it wasn't completely unknown. Sometimes there would be suspicious noises in locked rooms, and the soldiers on guard duty would be sent to investigate. They had always traced the disturbance to possums or dingoes that had got in from the desert. They'd never had people breaking in before – the base was too remote. But now two youths had been spotted in the main lab and were haring out of the side door into the desert.

Three guards were sent to the lab. As they rounded the corner by the lab entrance they caught sight of the two intruders. A male and a female in flying overalls. As they raced out of the door, the bright afternoon sunlight turned them into silhouettes. They ran like the devil was chasing them, their feet kicking up clouds of red dust. The way people run when they know they're in trouble.

Sergeant Kowalski and his two men pursued the pair a little way out into the scorching sunshine. They were racing towards the perimeter fence. The three soldiers stopped, steadied their AK-47s and fired a salvo of single rounds towards the perimeter fence. Plumes of dust rose as the bullets bit into the red sand.

The running figures changed direction abruptly like startled fish.

The sergeant spoke into a radio on his lapel. 'Sergeant Macy, stand by, they're heading your way. We're following from behind.'

'Roger,' came the reply.

Even though the base did not have intruder alerts very often, they still had protocols in case it happened.

Spies and saboteurs could do a lot of damage and had to be apprehended.

Sergeant Kowalski shipped his weapon back onto his shoulder, letting it hang casually on its sling. 'Take it easy, boys, we don't need to knock ourselves out. Look at 'em go. They won't be able to keep that up for long in this heat.'

Ben and Kelly were still running like the wind. Now they were alongside the dome. They were easy to spot – two tiny figures against a gleaming white background. They raced around the dome's curved perimeter until they were out of sight.

Kowalski spoke into his radio again. 'Macy, I think we can take our time. Where are they going to go? It's nothing but desert out there.'

About four hundred metres away, near the other entrance, Sergeant Macy's men were jogging towards the dome, ready to take up the chase. Like greyhounds on a racetrack, in a moment they would come running out the other side.

None of the soldiers noticed the cloud of dust blowing up on the other side of the dome. They didn't even take much notice of the noise – a tinny buzz like the engine of a lawnmower or a tiny boat.

But then a machine rose into the air above the dome. It was a spindly collection of struts like a First World War plane. Two figures sat in the tiny cockpit. The plane climbed, cleared the perimeter fence by a whisker and soared away into the blue sky.

The two GIs watched, speechless.

'Aw, nuts,' grunted Kowalski.

Chapter Nineteen

Bel had a searing headache. She trudged along past buildings that were blackened and dripping with water. They still smelled hot and the water was slowly turning to steam.

The whole street was blanketed in a thick smoky fog.

The road surface was soft under her feet like freshly baked cookies, and the metal rails of the tram tracks had expanded in the heat and burst out of the hilly tarmac.

Those tram lines might be what saved her, Bel thought. She knew that they ran towards the west side of town – and the sea. She couldn't see more than a few metres in front of her now, but she could follow the tram lines.

She passed a traffic light lying in the street, a vaguely oblong block of melted black plastic, with circles of red, amber and green, like a piece of sculpture by Salvador Dali.

The heat was making her head throb like a bass drum and the yellow protective coat didn't help. It was stiff and heavy to move in. Her entire body was running with sweat, her shirt and skirt wringing wet.

She angrily pulled open the coat's Velcro fastenings and took it off, but as soon as she did so, her back, chest and arms started to scorch. It felt as though she had peeled her own skin off. She put the coat back on, fastened it all the way to the top and walked on.

Ahead of her she saw a phone box – a mess of blackened plastic like a burned-out shower cubicle. The fire brigade had ringed it with yellow caution tape. That meant there was a body inside. Bel averted her gaze, but couldn't help catching a glimpse of what was inside. A blackened figure was hunched, bent over the phone. Bel knew from her work in other disaster areas that when somebody burned to death they curled up like a cooked prawn.

A noise behind her made her jump: it was the sound of a vehicle moving. She peered through the smoke and steam – was it coming towards her or going away? Red brake lights, enlarged to blobs by the smoky air, looked like a dot of colour on wet blotting paper. She started to run towards them, waving her arms.

'Hey! Help! Help!'

The driver of the army truck wanted to get out of the burning streets as fast as possible, but he had to be careful as debris kept looming out of the fog. He had a truck full of rescued civilians and the last thing he needed was to damage the truck and strand them all.

In the seats behind him, a bedraggled-looking group sat in a silent row. They looked like they had come from a set of Happy Families cards – a vet, a decorator, a postman, a jockey and two people wearing tattered golf clothes.

Victoria, Troy and their embattled companions had been rescued at last. By chance, they had run into the path of the rescue truck. They would look back on this as the day they'd beaten the odds.

But Bel wasn't so lucky. Victoria was gazing, exhausted, out of the back of the truck. The streets went past in a dream of fog. The heavy thrum of the truck's diesel engine was lulling her to sleep. She didn't hear the woman calling, just caught a brief glimpse of movement. She rubbed her eyes and looked again, but it was only a fluorescent yellow smudge in the gloom, a trick of the light. She settled back in her seat and closed her eyes.

Fate had flipped a coin.

Bel ran fast, but she couldn't run fast enough to catch the Jeep. The red gleam of the rear lights gradually dissolved into the smoky air. Bel's eyes were blurred with stinging smoke and her tears of desperation.

Suddenly, behind her, she heard a sound like the growl of a waking giant and a shockwave threw her to the ground. She landed heavily on her knees and elbows, and for a moment crouched, stunned with pain. When she looked, up the smoke hung around her so thickly, it was as though her face was draped in a grey curtain. There was a ringing in her ears and she became aware of a weight pressing down on her. As she moved, pieces of rubble slid off her back. Broken masonry was all around her: bricks and shattered concrete, black and greasy from fire.

What on earth had happened? Unable to take it in, she sat down amongst the rubble for a few moments, recovering from the shock.

The dust gradually settled, and when she turned and saw the scene behind her, Bel couldn't believe her eyes. Where moments before there had been a building, there was now a hole like a missing tooth. The façade had collapsed into the street. If Bel hadn't been running after the Jeep, she would have been right underneath it when it came down

Fate had flipped another coin.

Her ears were ringing so loudly she didn't notice the sound of her phone.

Up in the microlight, Ben looked at his phone in the hands-free cradle on the dashboard. The display gave the message he had been longing to see: '*Calling*'. The dialling tone came through strongly in his and Kelly's headsets.

They looked at each other, excited.

'A little more throttle,' said Kelly. Her voice was hushed, hardly daring to speak in case Bel's voice came through.

They were sharing control of the microlight while Kelly mapped out their route. She operated the pedals and kept her forearm on the stick, while Ben adjusted the throttle and tried the mobile phones.

'The lines must be back up,' said Kelly. 'She'll answer in a minute.'

She stiffened in her seat and looked down at the map and then out of the windscreen. 'Oh my goodness. That's Adelaide.'

A dark smudge had been growing on the horizon. At first it was barely noticeable – just a grey speck in the blue evening sky. But now it was getting wider, like ink spreading through the clouds.

Ben had a cold, ominous feeling. How much of the city had burned in order to turn such a big patch of sky dark like that? A story Bel had told him many years ago came back to him. She had been visiting some place after a volcano had erupted. He was too young to remember the details, but she had told him that the ash in the air turned the sky dark as night.

Bel's phone continued to ring unanswered, and as the microlight drew closer to the pall of smoke, its two passengers felt very uneasy.

'Where are we going to land?' asked Ben.

Kelly looked down at the map. 'There's an airfield a little way down the coast. We can head for there. It should be well away from the fire area.'

They were nearly safe, but Ben felt far from relieved. Why didn't Bel answer?

Kelly's phone rang. She automatically went to pick it up, then waved her bandaged hands in frustration. 'Quick! Answer it!'

Ben hooked his phone out of the cradle, put Kelly's in and pressed answer.

'*Kelly?*' It was the major's voice.

'Dad!' exclaimed Kelly. 'Where are you?'

'*In Melbourne. Where are you?*'

'Melbourne? Is that where the kidnappers have taken you?'

'*What kidnappers? I got picked up by the army.*'

Kelly and Ben exchanged puzzled looks. 'But you said some protestors had kidnapped you,' said Kelly. 'When you called me.'

'When I called you . . .? I only called you to see if you were all right. But, oh, you mean the protestors at the conference centre. I told you about them. But they weren't kidnappers. They tried to get a statement from me. One of them was a little crazy – he pulled a knife.'

'A knife! Dad . . .'

'I wasn't in any serious danger, sweetheart. He was just young and frustrated. I kept calm and let him boil off the worst of his anger, and once his friends started arguing with him he soon gave it up. Once they realized they weren't going to get me to say anything, they didn't hang around.'

Ben's phone was on his knee. It flashed up a message. 'Cannot connect'. He had been timed out. He stabbed the CALL button again. Would it work a second time? Had that been his only chance?

It started ringing again.

'So why,' Kelly was saying, 'did you call me and say you were on the Ghan?'

'The Ghan?' repeated the major. 'I didn't say that.' There was a pause as he obviously tried to remember what he did say. 'I was on the gantry outside. They *brought me out of an emergency exit onto the top of the fire escape. I was trying to let you know Bel needed help – she was still inside. Have you heard from her? Did she get out OK? I've been asking the fire department here but it's total confusion, as you'd expect.'*

Kelly looked over at Ben, who shook his head. Bel still wasn't answering.

'We're still trying to get in touch with her,' said Kelly.

'And where are you?'

'We're in the microlight. We're fine, we're safe.'

'Good. I've gotta go, sweetheart. Other people need this connection. See you later.' He cut the call.

Ben swapped the phones over in the cradle again. The sound of his phone ringing came through on their headsets.

'We were wasting our time chasing the Ghan,' he said. 'Meanwhile, my mum—'

He choked, unable to say more. Kelly couldn't think of any words. She was so relieved to hear from her father, but she could hardly say that. Not while Ben was worrying if his mother was alive or dead.

In any case they had other things to think about now. The black cloud was leaking into the sky around them, turning the deep blue to grey. The phone displays and the lights on the dashboard shone brighter. But when they looked away from the fire, the evening sky was still light. The immense pall of smoke was creating an effect like an eclipse.

'What's our plan?' said Ben, looking at the wall of smoke ahead of them. 'Go through the middle?'

'Are you nuts? It's heaving with thermals. We go around it. You'll have to take the stick – we need fine control. Move right and make sure we don't lose speed and height.'

Ben guided the plane to the right while Kelly balanced with the pedals.

'We have to be very, very careful,' said Kelly. 'Even this far out from the city, we could still be hit with thermals.'

The smoke formed a definite column to their left, like a charcoal tower in the clouds.

As they concentrated on the view, they had almost tuned out the ringing sound from Ben's phone, but suddenly it was answered.

'*Ben? Where have you been?*' Bel's voice sounded hoarse and rasping.

'Mum!' Ben's heart leaped. 'I've been ringing you for ages. Where are you?'

'*I'm on the roof of the tram terminus.*'

'Where's that?'

'*It's in the middle of Adelaide. I was trying to get out to the coast but I went the wrong way. I can't get out.*'

The middle of Adelaide. She was still right in the heart of the inferno!

'Mum,' said Ben, 'I'm coming to get you. I'm in the microlight. I can fly in.'

Kelly was getting this on her headset too. 'We can't do that,' she spluttered.

Bel heard her voice. '*Is that you, Kelly? You can't come and get me in a microlight. I'm stuck on a roof. It's twenty metres long. You can't land a microlight on a roof. It's not like one of your computer games, Ben.*'

Ben interrupted. 'Mum, I don't think it's anything like a computer game.'

Kelly took over the conversation. 'Stay where you

are, Dr Kelland. We'll send help. The roof of the tram terminus, right?'

'*Right*,' said Bel. '*And be quick. I don't know how long this building will last.*'

Ben cut the call and dialled 000. '*Lines are busy*,' droned the recorded message.

Suddenly the microlight dropped like a stone, flipping their stomachs. They had hit the thermals.

Ben had forgotten how bad that felt. His buttocks left the seat and the seat belt pressed into his lap. For a moment he was floating. The top of his head hit the roof of the cockpit, and his stomach seemed to join it.

They emerged from a cloud into bright sunshine again, flying along smoothly. Down below was the sea, and the west coast of Adelaide. In the gaps between the dark clouds Ben could see hundreds of boats bobbing on the water – boats where people had taken refuge. Further inland, the city was a mass of black clouds, dotted with huge flickers of orange like burning coals.

Ben dialled 000 again. The display continued to say the same message: *Lines are busy*.

'We've dropped forty feet,' said Kelly. 'Pull up.'

Instead of climbing as she had instructed him, Ben pushed the nose of the microlight down.

Kelly shrieked, 'Are you crazy? I said *up*!'

Ben kept his hands firmly on the controls and they bumped along for a few more minutes. When he was next able to gather his thoughts and speak, his voice was grim. 'The tram terminal's in the centre of town, right? It's just a ten-minute ride from the coast. I looked it up when I was waiting in the hotel. Well, ten minutes in a tram is barely a couple of minutes in the air. We can go there ourselves.'

'No,' said Kelly firmly. She groaned as the microlight dropped again, but Ben managed to anticipate and accelerated out of the dive.

Once he'd steadied the plane, Ben hit redial on his phone, but still the display gave the same message. *Lines are busy.*

He waved a hand at his phone. 'Look at that. We can't get through to the emergency services. If we try and go for help, it will take ages for anyone to get to her – we may be flying over her head right now.'

Kelly swallowed, then spoke slowly and deliberately, as though explaining something to a dim child. 'You can't land in the town, Ben. The buildings will set up thermals and cross-winds everywhere.'

Ben circled the plane round. It was now possible to distinguish the shapes of buildings in the blackened mass below. He could feel the heat radiating up from them. Sweat ran down his forehead and back.

'We're at four hundred feet,' he said. 'I'm going to start looking for a place to land. Do you think I should be higher or lower?'

Kelly refused to answer.

This was absolutely typical of Bel, thought Ben. She marched through life without a thought for the emotional wreckage she left behind – like she had when she walked out on him and his dad. Whenever he tried to spend time with her, he got into terrible scrapes. He knew it hadn't been her *fault*, but last summer he'd gone to London to see her and ended up fighting for his life in a flood! Hell and high water, he thought grimly. Well, he'd done high water; now it was time for hell.

'Kelly, my mother is down there. I am taking this plane down, one way or another. Do you want me to guess what to do and make a mess of it, or will you help?'

Kelly spoke in a small voice. 'Keep at this height, but increase your speed a little so we've got the power in case we need to climb.'

She was no longer fighting him. She had given in. In a way that made Ben more nervous, but he couldn't let Kelly see that, otherwise she'd take over and make him abort the plan. He had to seem confident and determined. For all their sakes.

Chapter Twenty

Ben watched their height drop steadily on the altimeter, then glanced out of the window. The ground was a mass of dark cloud. Some buildings were still burning, throwing flames and smoke high into the sky. He was surprised by how smooth their descent was. Maybe the buildings were all the same temperature and weren't throwing out the isolated currents that played havoc with the plane. It wasn't that there were no thermals; more that the town was now just one giant furnace.

As if wanting to punish him for his optimism, the microlight lurched upwards. Ben gritted his teeth and waited for the sickening sensation to pass.

'I told you the thermals would be bad,' said Kelly.

'Just find me somewhere to land,' said Ben. The plane began to wobble like a trembling hand.

Kelly looked out of the window. 'Let's take a look at that park. It's quite close to the tram station. Turn left.'

Ben shifted the controls correctly but the microlight soared upwards again as it caught another thermal.

When they stabilized once more, Kelly let out her breath slowly. 'Go back down to four hundred feet and take the plane around in a big circle. Careful of your speed.'

Ben dipped one wing so that the microlight banked. He saw blue lights moving under the smoke layer, flashes of red and silver fire engines, and the shimmer of the firemen's turnout gear reflecting in the evening sun. It was like the metallic glint of fish in murky water.

Kelly let out a loud sigh. 'I can't see – there's too much smoke. We'll have to go in closer. It's not very safe but I've got to see what's on the ground. Don't even think of trying to land this time – this is our reconnaissance pass.' She checked the instruments and waved a bandaged hand. 'The turn has slowed you – I told you it would. More throttle or we'll stall.'

Ben took the plane down to 200 feet. They flew over the park. A few bare trees reached spindly limbs up into the smoke. The grass was not visible at all.

Kelly shook her head. 'Those trees will get in the way.'

'Can't we steer between them?' said Ben.

'We'll be coming in at sixty knots – that's a hundred and ten kilometres per hour. You can't steer at that speed. If you clip a wing we'll turn over. We've got to find somewhere else.'

'What about down there?' said Ben. He pointed down to a wide street. The smoke cleared for a moment, revealing abandoned cars and an overturned market stall. 'Er – don't bother to answer that,' he added, and turned the plane away.

As he started to climb again, he spotted the perfect landing site below. It was a long dual carriageway, with three lanes on each side, leading away from the centre of town over the river Torrens.

'There!' he exclaimed.

'Ben, that's a bridge. There's a parapet in the

middle and wires on each side. That's a crazy idea.'

'You said you'd landed on a bridge before,' countered Ben.

'I've never done anything of the sort,' she retorted.

'You were telling me earlier that you landed a plane on a bridge in Seattle.'

'I was just the passenger. I was sitting in the back, scared stiff.'

The windscreen was suddenly full of seagulls rushing towards them. Their wingspan made them look huge. Kelly ducked and shrieked and Ben pressed back in his seat.

There was a bang as something hit the wing, then a seagull thudded onto the windscreen like roadkill. As it tumbled away, it left a smear of blood.

'We got one,' grinned Ben, trying to act flippant to cover his shock.

The grin was soon wiped off his face. The whole cockpit began to shake, the engine vibrated and the plane was drifting. 'Hey, Kelly . . .'

Kelly looked up, fury in her eyes. 'That bird must have nicked our propeller. The engine's pulling us to the side. Get your feet away.'

She tried the pedals but they didn't respond, so she went for more brutal tactics. She pulled the stick hard to one side and rammed the right pedal down.

The plane swung dramatically sideways, slicing downwards through the air. They flew so close over a telegraph pole that Ben could see the grain of the wood. Then, as they tilted, he could see only sky out of the window.

'Turn the engine off,' shouted Kelly. 'It's pulling us about too much.'

Ben thought she must have gone mad. '*What?*'

Kelly shouted louder. 'Turn the engine off!'

Ben turned the key. Red lights came on all across the instrument panel and the needle on the rev counter dropped to zero. The plane was eerily quiet. Kelly used the pedals to level the plane and he could hear the rudder move on the tail.

'Shall I start it up?' said Ben. After all, the time-honoured way of solving a mechanical problem was to switch a machine off and then switch it on again.

'No, the propeller will tear off if we do that. We'll have to come down like a glider.'

'Come down where?' said Ben.

Kelly's voice was weak, as though she could scarcely believe what she was saying. 'The bridge.'

Ben swallowed, his heart thumping.

'Start your approach. Turn and line up with the middle lane on the left-hand side. And get it right. We don't have an engine to get us out of trouble so there are no second chances.'

Ben took the controls gingerly. Without the engine noise he could hear every creak in the microlight's frame. When he moved the pedals it was even worse: they made thumping noises in the floor and behind him. When he used the stick it made the whole wing move.

'Ben,' shouted Kelly, 'stop being so feeble! Fly the darned thing!'

Carefully he lined up the plane on the road. The river was in the middle of his horizon – a murky ribbon growing bigger by the second. The town was beyond. A pall of wet smoke blew towards them. It was like trying to catch your breath inside a wet towel.

'Get the nose down more,' said Kelly. 'Stop looking downwards – look at where you're planning to stop.'

Their height was 70 feet and the road filled Ben's

windscreen now. His palms were slick with sweat on the controls.

Like when they had landed in the desert before, everything on the ground started getting big; everything except the bridge, which looked like a very small target indeed, a hump of tarmac with some thin white lines marking out the traffic lanes. It would be easy to misjudge it and end up in the river. And the river didn't look like a friendly place to land. It was full of debris, some still burning, some sooty and black – all of it charging along in the current like a mad boat race.

'Nose up,' said Kelly. 'Or we'll keep gathering speed and bulldoze into the ground.'

Ben tweaked the stick back and the microlight see-sawed backwards. Without the engine noise he had completely lost his feel for the craft.

Kelly growled in irritation and elbowed the stick forward. The nose pointed down again. The road surface was so close they could see dark smears of tyre rubber on the white lines.

Kelly's face was grim with concentration. 'Nose up slowly.'

Ben followed her instructions and there was a bump as the back wheels hit the road.

'We're down,' said Kelly. 'Stick forward. Brake on.'

Ben squeezed the brake. Lampposts and signs whizzed past at a frightening speed. Coming in at 110 kilometres per hour had been scary enough in the desert, but in a built-up area it felt positively suicidal. Ben was braking, but the road surface was slick with water and the tyres had no friction.

The bridge led into a roundabout. Ahead was a black and white chevron sign. There was no way they would stop in time. 'Oh no!' gasped Kelly.

'I'll have to steer around it!' yelled Ben. He pulled the plane hard left.

And Kelly pumped the pedals hard right.

The microlight skidded on the wet road and slid sideways past a row of burned-out cars.

'Don't you know which way to go round a round-about?' yelled Ben.

'We don't have roundabouts in the States,' retorted Kelly.

Water and oil were smeared all over the road, turning it into a skating rink. The plane skidded forwards, jolting its two passengers with every bump in the road, and Ben visualized the spindly undercarriage hitting a pothole and snapping. He tried the brake but the wheels had locked. They would just have to wait until the microlight slowed down by itself.

Behind the cars was a burned-out building. Soot streaked its white façade; its windows were blackened holes and pockets of orange fire still glowed in its interior. The building next to it was still burning, pumping dark smoke into the sky

Kelly tried to grab Ben's arm with her mittened hand. 'Ben, look!'

Ben followed her gaze and his blood ran cold.

Two doors along from the burning building was a petrol station. So far the flames hadn't reached it, but it would only take one stray spark to ignite the whole thing.

And the microlight was heading straight towards it.

Ben grasped the stick firmly and squeezed the brake. The wheels were still locked. Nothing happened.

He unfastened his seat belt, then reached across and undid Kelly's. 'We've got to bale out – now.'

She held up her hands, helpless. 'I can't open my door.'

'Come out my side.' Ben flicked open the door catch.

Kelly looked down at the road, an expression of horror on her face. She looked like she had frozen.

'Don't be so feeble!' yelled Ben. He clambered awkwardly out of the cockpit, then leaned back in to grab Kelly by the scruff of her neck and drag her across to the opening. She came out backwards, her bandaged hands painfully smacking into the ground as she half-fell, half-climbed out of the plane. Ben rolled on the tarmac, then got straight to his feet, easing the pain from his bashed elbows and knees. Kelly crouched on the ground, her eyes on the microlight, her hands tucked under her armpits.

The plane crunched side on into a yellow rubbish skip. The metal frame bent like wire and the taut wing material tore loose to hang down in ribbons. The steel cables that held the entire structure together from pedals to rudder snapped, whipping into the air. The cables swung into the Perspex cockpit and shattered it.

Ben winced. 'Oops. I'm glad we weren't inside when that happened. Did you have it insured?'

'You're not even old enough to know what insurance is.' Kelly sat up and gazed around at the smoking buildings. 'Talk about out of the frying pan . . . How do you propose we're going to get out of here? Or find your mother, come to that.'

'We can get out on the river. I know how to drive a boat.'

'Yeah? Better than you fly a plane, I hope.' Kelly got to her feet. As she did so, something fell out of her pocket; she tried to catch it, but it slipped out of her bandaged hands and hit the tarmac. Her phone. She gave Ben an appealing look.

He shook his head. 'Surely you don't trust me to pick it up for you – I might break it,' he said crossly. 'After all, I'm really useless, according to you.'

'Please. I'm sure you're great with boats. And your flying's really not too bad.'

Ben picked up the phone and tried to dial Bel. His own had been left in the plane. Kelly's picture of the red and pink power chute glowed but the keyboard didn't respond.

'I think it's broken.'

'Oh *great*!' Kelly stamped her foot. If she could have grabbed the phone in her bandaged mittens, she looked about ready to throw it in the river.

But Ben had an idea. He turned the phone display towards Kelly. 'You bought one of these chute things this morning, didn't you. Where's the shop?'

'Whitmoor Square. It's just over there by the park we tried to land in.'

He slipped the phone back into her pocket. 'That's where we're going. We'll get some of those chute things, pick Mum up, and then head out towards the sea.' He started running in the direction of the park.

Kelly set off after him. 'I thought you were going to get a boat.'

'I don't see any boats,' said Ben. 'And we can't take a boat up on the tram station roof.'

As Ben ran, he saw something he really didn't like. The fire from the burning building had spread. Already the offices next door to the petrol station were ablaze. It was only a matter of time before the petrol tanks caught. Then the whole place was going to go sky high.

Chapter Twenty-one

Ben was a good runner. Being tall for his age, he usually made good times on the athletics field. Kelly seemed to be pretty fit too and she had no trouble keeping up. They set off at a good pace down a road lined with dripping, black buildings.

As they ran, waves of heat pressed against them on all sides like a wall and thick drifts of smoke clogged their lungs. Coughing, Ben stopped for a moment and waited with hands on knees. Sprinting was easy enough in clean air, but it wasn't so easy when you had to hold your breath.

He looked round and saw Kelly staggering along.

She looked as though she had already run a marathon. He leaned on an abandoned car to try and get his breath, and saw through the window that there was a bottle of water and a navy blue sweatshirt on the passenger seat. He pulled open the door, grabbed the sweatshirt and ripped it in two. He seized the water and poured it out over the material, then ran back to Kelly.

He took her by the elbow and held the wet material up to her face. 'I'm going to tie this on your face like a mask,' he said. 'You'll find it easier to breathe.' His words came out in gasps between the drifting clouds of smoke. He also wanted to warn her that the petrol station was going to blow, but he didn't have the breath.

She nodded, and stood while he fastened the material behind her head. Then he held the other piece over his mouth and started to run. Kelly followed, her eyes over the top of the mask wide with fear.

A fire-engine siren reverberated between the build-ings. Ben looked round, expecting to see a truck heading towards them, but then realized it must have been a few streets away. The damp air magnified the sound.

As he set off again, he looked at the burned-out buildings – they were straight out of a nightmare. A thought occurred to him and he wished it hadn't – would the shop they were looking for still be there? Or would the flames have already gutted it?

Kelly buffeted him with her bandaged hand. 'Not that way; over here.' The mask had slipped down around her neck. She tried to push it up as she led the way into a shopping precinct.

'Here,' gasped Kelly. She bent over double, struggling to get her breath in the smoke-clogged air.

Even breathing through the wet material, Ben felt like his lungs would burst. His eyes were streaming with tears from the smoke. Slowly the shop in front of him came into focus.

It hadn't been burned. But it had been looted.

The big glass window was shattered. He stepped in over fallen dummies, rucksacks and boots. Tiny shards of glass crunched under his feet. But at least it wasn't filled with smoke and breathing was easier.

'What a mess,' Kelly said as she followed him inside.

Clothes had been pulled off the rails and shoeboxes lay scattered all over the floor.

Ben didn't know where to start. 'Where did they keep the power chutes?'

Kelly squatted down beside a dummy on the floor. 'It was here. Someone took it.' She suddenly sounded close to tears.

Ben had a terrible sinking feeling. They had burned their bridges coming here – and now, it seemed, not only was there no way to get to Bel; they had no escape route themselves.

He saw a door to a stockroom at the back of the shop and hurried across, trampling over a pile of discarded jackets. Kelly seemed dangerously close to giving up: he had to keep them both going. 'They wouldn't just have the one on display,' he called. 'Come and help me look.'

The stockroom was piled high with boxes. Kelly appeared beside him and pointed at a high shelf. 'Up there! That's what you want.' There was hope in her voice again.

Ben climbed up the shelves and saw a stack of boxes with a picture of a power chute on the side. They were heavy and he had to brace his feet on the lower shelf before grabbing the boxes with both hands and pulling. Several boxes came out at once. Kelly dodged out of the way as they avalanched to the floor. Ben jumped down and passed one to her, then picked one up for himself.

They hurried back to the front window, their feet skating on the shattered glass. 'We'll have to put them on outside otherwise the chute will get tangled up,' Kelly told Ben. She reached the pavement and put the box down, then stopped, all the fight gone out of her.

'What's the matter?' said Ben, laying his box down next to hers.

'I just realized. They don't keep them fuelled in the shop.' She looked at him, tears in her eyes. 'Where are we going to get any gas?' After the strain of the past few hours, she was exhausted.

Ben felt exhausted too, but one thing he'd inherited from his mother: he didn't know how to quit. He spotted an old Land Rover, crusted with outback mud, parked at the end of the precinct. Like the shops, it had escaped fire damage. 'We'll get petrol out of that—'

Kelly shook her head. 'No good. The chutes need a two-stroke mix, like the microlight. We could have got it back at the gas station . . .' Her words trailed off.

Ben looked around, desperate for inspiration. Above the roofs, he could see a pall of black smoke in the direction they'd come from. Was it coming from the building next to the petrol station? It was certainly burning fiercely.

They had to keep going, he told himself firmly. They couldn't give up.

'You get the chutes ready,' he said, 'and I'll worry about the fuel.'

A look of horror came over Kelly's face. She laid a bandaged hand on his arm. 'Be careful.'

Ben set off at a run, back towards the petrol station. Hot smoke smothered him like a filthy wet blanket. Even when he held the wet material over his face it didn't seem to make much difference, but he forced himself to keep running. He had to get to the petrol station before the flames from the office building did.

His brain was working even faster than his legs. He needed a plan. As soon as he got to the roundabout, he'd be able to see whether he could safely reach the petrol station. If he was in any doubt, he'd turn round and come back.

It was a crazy plan. But without the fuel for the power chutes they couldn't get out of the city, which was worse.

He ran across the green and had to break stride to avoid tripping over something lying in his path. He almost failed to see it in the smoke.

He continued for a few paces, then stopped and looked back. It was a lawnmower.

Kelly had got the chutes laid out on the ground. They looked like giant flowers – one blue and lime-green, the other purple and pink. She looked up when she heard the screech of metal scraping over paving slabs. Ben was dragging the lawnmower noisily back towards her.

'Here's our fuel. Lawnmowers use a two-stroke mix, don't they? We need something to put it in.' He dashed through the broken shop window, grabbed a billycan from the camping display, took it to the lawnmower and tipped the fuel out.

'The fuel cap for the power pack is on the top,' said Kelly.

Now Ben saw the power packs for the first time; they looked like giant fans on metal frames, with a mass of straps and clips. Kelly had stood them upright, ready for use.

As he poured the viscous liquid into the fuel tanks, Ben glanced up at the roofline and the black smoke beyond the burning offices. If he hadn't found the lawnmower he might be there now.

Ben tossed the billycan away. 'Ready.'

Kelly crouched down beside one of the engines. 'Pull that red cord to start the engine, then put it on my back. Fasten everything tightly. It's basically a parachute harness with an industrial-strength fan attached.'

Ben shook his head, confused. 'You want me to start it and *then* put it on your back? Not the other way round?'

'That's just the way it's done,' said Kelly. 'Now hurry up.'

Ben pulled the cord. The engine roared into life and the white propeller inside its frame quickly became a blur. He fastened the harness around Kelly's waist and chest, then she got to her feet. Red webbing straps dangled between her legs. Ben fastened those too.

'Attach the two clips from the chute to my shoulders and put my hands through the steering loops – those red things by the harness,' Kelly told him.

Ben did that, then hooked the throttle cord through the harness so she could reach it with her teeth.

'It should be easy to see the tram station when we're in the air,' he said. A sudden thought occurred to him. 'Can these things carry two people?'

Kelly thought for a moment. 'They can take a sixteen-stone man and your mom must weigh less than half that. I weigh eight stone so I should be able to take her. She can cling to me.'

Above the trees, the plume of smoke continued to boil. It was getting bigger and darker.

Ben started his engine, put it on his back and set up his harness and controls. The spinning propeller reverberated through the metal frame to his very bones.

'Ready?' said Kelly.

Ben nodded.

'Do what I do. When the chute inflates, pull on the

throttle and take your feet off the ground.' She took the throttle between her teeth, then set off at a run down the street.

The lime-green chute flared out behind her like the train of a wedding dress. Ben followed the trailing material, making sure to leave enough room for her to get clear ahead of him. Just as he thought it would never get off the ground, the breeze caught the chute and started to lift it. Kelly opened the throttle. The engine roared. To Ben's amazement, her feet left the ground.

Ben felt the chute pull at his shoulders. He glanced behind. The pink material was fluttering up into the air. He pulled on the throttle. The chute filled with air and pulled him upwards. In moments he was soaring into the sky.

It was an amazing feeling. Flying the microlight had been fun but this was ten times better. It was so free, he felt like a bird. If only the engine was quieter it would be perfect.

Kelly climbed in a circling pattern. Ben copied her. The chute was easy to steer – just pull the cord and you went in that direction. In moments they were hanging above the roofs. Smoke blew past in drifting clouds. Through it they caught a glimpse of chimneys and steep roofs. The burning offices by the petrol station were completely obscured by a black pool of smoke.

Where was the tram station? Ben wondered. He had lost his bearings. He could see abandoned vehicles and fire engines, but no trams. The roofs around them were a mass of geometric shapes in tones of grey and black. He tried to slow down, so that he could hover in one place and get a proper look at the ground.

Suddenly a thermal shot him up twenty feet. He gunned the throttle to regain control. So that explained why Kelly was circling constantly.

He looked down. He was flying over the petrol station. The wind was now blowing the black smoke away, revealing the low white roof over the forecourt. It was surrounded by a sinister border of orange flames.

They had to find Bel quickly. If the petrol tanks under the station forecourt went up, they would be engulfed in the fireball like insects in a flame.

Then Ben caught sight of something below him.

Down in the murk, a bright yellow smudge beneath the cloud of smoke. It was moving. No . . . waving.

Ben eased up on the throttle and went down.

The yellow smudge took shape. It was a small red-headed figure waving a bright yellow fireman's jacket.

'Mum!' yelled Ben.

She was standing on a long, low roof lined with metal walkways and rows of skylights. That was obviously the tram station.

As she saw him she started waving more frantically.

Ben craned his neck and spotted Kelly's lime-green chute circling a short distance away. Ben flew up to get her attention, then headed back to the tram station roof – where Bel was now waving the jacket with a vigour bordering on fury. Ben cracked a smile as he saw her shouting up at him. When he flew off, she must have thought he hadn't seen her.

Ben flew in a small circle over the roof. Kelly was right behind him. She cut the revs of her engine to a gentle chug, and flared the pulleys on her chute so that she floated gently down.

Bel saw she was about to be rescued. She put the jacket on and looked up expectantly, but Kelly suddenly pulled the throttle and rose up again, away from the roof.

She manoeuvred her chute over until she was hovering opposite Ben. He shook his head, baffled, trying to mime, *What's going on?*

Kelly indicated her bandaged hands.

So what? thought Ben. Then understanding dawned. Kelly couldn't hold onto Bel and operate her chute at the same time.

Ben nodded. He would have to go down and get Bel himself.

He cut the revs and the chute began to drift slowly down. But would his chute be able to lift both of them? Ben figured he must be a lot heavier than Kelly.

Bel was glaring up at him, hands on hips, annoyed. Her blue eyes flashed in her grimy face. He saw her mouth something that was probably the sort of thing a thirteen-year-old shouldn't hear his mother saying.

Ben was aiming to land next to her but an air current took him over to the other side of the roof and deposited him on the glass canopy. Still partly supported by the chute, he had no choice but to run along the glass roof. At any moment he expected to crash through the panes, but obviously they were stronger than they looked. He half ran, half flew over to where Bel was standing.

'Mum, quick,' he gasped. 'Hook your arms into my harness.'

He expected Bel to obey immediately, but instead she looked at him with a sceptical expression.

Behind her he could see the plume of smoke rising from the petrol station. It was getting darker as the thick smoke shut out the light from the setting sun.

'Ben,' she said, 'you surely don't expect that thing to carry the both of us?'

Typical! Ben thought. Here he was, risking his life, and his mother – just as she used to do when he did anything dubious as a small child – seemed to be *angry*, rather than worried about him. What was it with parents? How come they just slipped into telling-off mode in any situation?

'I didn't have time to pack a spare!' he almost screamed at her.

The more he lost his temper, the more Bel dug her heels in. He forced himself to speak very calmly. 'Let's say we've got a fifty-fifty chance. Could be worse.'

Bel still looked dubious, but she took a step towards him.

'Hurry!' he yelled.

At last Bel seemed to understand it was an emergency. She turned round so that she faced forward and put her arms into his harness. Ben unfastened the waist band and adjusted it so it would go around her too. Hastily he buckled her in front of him. She smelled of wet soot and smoke, and chemicals.

'Now what?' said Bel.

'Now we have to run like blazes!'

It was awkward, like running in one of those races where you're tied to someone else.

The chute began to catch the air and rose, dragging upwards on his shoulders. Ben pulled on the throttle. The engine roared, but it didn't pull them into the air. Something was wrong.

The chute didn't have enough power to lift them.

Chapter Twenty-two

Ben tried to slow down, but Bel was powering forwards, pulling him along by the harness. He yelled in her ear, 'Stop!'

Bel stumbled to a halt and he nearly fell over her.

'What did you do that for?' she snapped.

'You're too heavy,' Ben gasped. He unclipped the waist harness and Bel half fell forward.

She twisted round and looked at him, furious. Her red hair was nearly black with sweat and soot. In fact most of her was. 'Don't be so rude.'

'It's that jacket. You'll have to take it off.' With one

hand he yanked the jacket off her shoulders, then saw her boots.

'Take those off too,' he said, pointing. 'They must weigh five pounds each! Jesus, Mum, you picked a hell of a time to give up wearing sandals.'

'Take off my boots?' said Bel. 'Have you gone mad?'

'Yes, and take mine off too. Otherwise we won't be able to get airborne.'

She knelt down, obviously not convinced he was entirely sane.

'Try and do it sometime today,' shouted Ben. 'There's a petrol station over there and it's about to blow.'

'There's no need for sarcasm,' she said. But the thought of an exploding petrol station obviously persuaded her. She undid his bootlaces, grumbling, 'I haven't done this to you since you were three years old. Foot up.'

Ben lifted his foot. 'Yeah, yeah,' he muttered.

She got one boot off, then the other. The sky was growing darker and darker.

Ben saw Kelly, a lime-green figure high in the grey

clouds. She was already making good progress towards the sea.

Bel knelt down and unfastened her own boots. She had done them up securely with double knots because they were a size too big.

While she fumbled with them, Ben watched the roof of the petrol station. The flames were getting higher and burning debris was dropping down onto the fore-court. Then a chunk of blazing roof fabric landed near one of the pumps.

'Hurry up!' yelled Ben.

'I'm going as fast as I can,' grumbled Bel.

'Well, go faster,' retorted Ben, 'or we've had it.'

The piece of roof was throwing out flames and sparks barely half a metre away from the looped hose of the pump. Ben watched the progress of the flames with the same fascination that a mouse watches a cat stalk towards it.

Bel stood up, both boots off. She turned her back to Ben and hooked her arms into the shoulder straps. Ben again fastened the waistband and the leg straps.

'You know the routine,' he shouted. 'On your marks . . . *go!*'

The roof was covered in fine gravel and it was painful to run on it in bare feet. Ben felt Bel falter with the discomfort and yelled in her ear, 'Faster!'

The chute rose up behind. He opened the throttle. The propeller roared up to top speed.

Had they shed enough weight? Would the chute's remaining fuel be enough to lift them?

The power pack dragged their feet clear of the roof, but it was like a badly judged take-off with too little lift. Ben kept the throttle on maximum. It wasn't enough. They were starting to drift back down again.

Ben saw a flash out of the corner of his eye. Suddenly they shot vertically up into the air as if they'd been fired out of a cannon. The deafening roar came a split second later. A wave of heat followed, so intense that Ben felt as if his skin was peeling off. The shock wave catapulted them further up still. The sky around them was completely dark and filled with burning debris that wheeled and tumbled like a flock of birds on fire.

The flames had reached the petrol tanks in the filling station. The explosion and the immense burst of heat had rocketed them vertically upwards. Far below, under the seething black smoke, the petroleum fire blazed as bright as the sun.

Way off in the distance, Ben could see a lime-green speck. It must be Kelly. She seemed to already be well away from the danger. That told him which way to steer to reach the coast.

He pulled on the left side of the canopy, but the chute didn't respond. He looked up. Was the steering rope caught?

Then he saw a tongue of orange flame licking at the purple fabric. One section of his canopy was a tattered scrap of smouldering material. Already he could see sky through a hole that was getting wider by the second.

Quickly, he pulled the other side. The chute responded and took him inland again, over the burning city. Now they were starting to lose height again.

Bel twisted her head and looked round at him in alarm. She spotted the hole in the canopy and her face froze in horror.

They caught another thermal and the chute soared up once more. The burning city shrank to toy size. The intense heat dissipated and Ben felt able to breathe again. Ahead, the horizon opened out and the smoke started to disperse. He could see the sea.

But did they have enough lift to get all the way there?

Now he could make out the jetty and, beyond it, the harbour. Boats covered almost every square metre of the water's surface. People were crowded onto the decks, huddling together as they watched their city burn.

A crash landing in the harbour wouldn't be so bad. Except that Ben wasn't at all sure they were going to make it that far.

They were losing altitude again and he tried to open the throttle, but it was already at maximum. The hole in the chute above them was widening as the fabric continued to smoulder.

They passed over burning roofs, then a burning park, drifting lower all the time. Leaves from the trees lining the park threw sparks into the air.

They continued to descend, their feet brushing over flaming branches. Whirling cinders burned their bare soles.

Ben smelled scorching fabric and looked up.

Another section of the chute had gone. He gave it another thirty seconds at most then the power pack would be blasting air up with no chute to catch it.

They didn't need thirty seconds. When Ben looked down again, they were sailing over the boats. They'd made it. He cut the engine. The silence was immediate and almost soothing.

But now they were falling with only a small chute like a tattered umbrella to slow their descent.

The mast of a yacht loomed up and Bel pulled her feet out of the way. Ben, reacting slower, took a painful bang to his shins. They came down even lower and passed over a large white cabin cruiser. Their feet scrabbled along the top, leaving grubby marks. They passed over another boat and Ben tried to slow them down, extending his legs to brace his feet on the cabin roof, but his bare soles slipped on it.

Still they carried on, over another cruiser, getting lower all the time.

A dinghy crossed their path. The people in it were waving and shouting at them, but there was nothing Ben could do to get out of their way. The passengers threw themselves to opposite ends of the dinghy as the four-footed purple flying creature ran through the middle of their boat.

The next thing in their path was a striped awning on a yacht. The roofs of the cabins had been solid. This was canvas, like a tent. It bent under their weight; then, with a loud crack, one of the poles supporting the awning gave way. The canvas roof turned into a slide, and Ben and Bel found themselves tumbling towards a large square of sapphire blue.

The yacht's swimming pool.

They hit the water with a splash. Fortunately the water wasn't deep. Ben managed to stand up and unfasten the waist band. Wet purple fabric clung to their heads like a clammy skin as he and Bel battled to get out of the harness.

When Ben had fought his way out of the chute, he saw a row of people in swimsuits and sun hats. They were all holding drinks and looking at the new arrivals in astonishment.

He swam to the side of the pool. A bronzed Australian girl with pink-streaked blonde hair smiled down at him. 'Are you OK?' she asked.

Bel emerged from the other end of the chute. Her

face was streaked with soot and her red hair was a tangled mess. She waded to the steps at the end of the pool and climbed out, her hand outstretched to introduce herself.

'Er – sorry about dropping in unannounced. Hi. I'm Dr Bel Kelland and this is my son Ben.'

A man in a peaked cap put his drink down and went to help her. 'Did you come from the city?'

Bel nodded. Water made sooty pools around her bare feet.

One of the women picked up a blue towel, put it around Bel's shoulders and invited her to sit on a sun lounger.

Suddenly there was a titanic boom and for a moment everyone looked at each other. It was so loud, it shook the sky overhead. Was it another explosion from the city? It seemed incredible – the sound was louder than a hundred petrol stations blowing up. Then the penny dropped.

'It's thunder!' said the girl with the pink-streaked hair.

The heavens opened and rain came down. It was real summer storm rain, lashing down onto the deck in great, fat, splashy drops. The woman hurried Bel inside, while the girl helped Ben drag the chute and the soaked engine out of the pool.

He didn't go in immediately. He stood on the sun deck, marvelling at the feel of rain on his hot skin . . .

Chapter Twenty-three

Ben walked down the corridor, a bunch of flowers in one hand, looking for room 319. The private hospital in Melbourne didn't smell like a hospital, or even look much like one. With its pale yellow walls and pastel-coloured paintings it seemed more like a hotel. At the moment, filled with an overspill of patients from other hospitals, it was like a hotel that had been seriously overbooked.

He found the room and knocked. He heard the TV being silenced and then a voice called out, 'Come in.' The voice was American. It sounded hoarse.

Ben walked in.

'Oh, it's you.'

Kelly was sitting up in bed. The bandages on her hands looked a bit cleaner than the last time Ben had seen her. There was an oxygen mask hanging from a rail above the bed. As usual, she was anything but pleased to see him.

'I brought you some flowers,' said Ben, 'but now I wish I hadn't. I'll give them to the orphan next door.'

'They don't have an orphan next door,' croaked Kelly. 'They have a hunky rock star. Why don't you go and send him in here and you can go and sit in his room on your own.'

'Why do you get a room to yourself?' said Ben. 'Did you tell them you're a rock star?'

'It's for security reasons. Half the world seems to think Uncle Sam is responsible for war, famine and the global recession. Given the trouble my dad had with those protestors yesterday, the authorities figured I could use a little extra privacy.'

'You're lucky you're not in a jail cell for wasting police time. I hear they sent two helicopters to intercept the Ghan.'

'Yeah, well, it was an honest mistake. And they

don't have time to worry about that with everything else that's happened—'

Talking made her cough. She tried to grab a tube dangling down from a water container above the bed, but instead of pulling it towards her, her bandaged hands only succeeded in batting it away. Cursing, she tried to retrieve it.

Ben let her struggle for a moment, then his better nature took over. He reached over and moved the tube so that she could reach it. She sucked on it, then let it fall from her mouth.

'Thanks,' she said grudgingly, then started coughing. 'It's smoke inhalation. They say it'll pass in a day or two. How come you're not suffering with it, anyway?'

'I don't open my mouth as often as you do, I guess.' Ben realized he was still holding the flowers, so he dropped them on the table at the end of the bed. They landed with a slap. He nodded at the saline bag hanging beside her bed, and the line leading into her arm. 'So what's with the drip?'

'My burns got infected. Something to do with not keeping them clean, running around in the desert all afternoon, then landing in the sea and being hauled out by some guys who'd been gutting fish and hadn't washed their hands. So now I'm on mega-strong antibiotics. Why are you here?'

Ben shrugged. 'We're staying in the hotel next door. There's nothing on TV except *The Towering Inferno* and I didn't fancy that. I heard you were here and thought I'd see what you were up to.'

Kelly began to laugh, a dry sound like a seal barking. 'Yeah, well, I'm not your babysitter any more. Run along now and let me be miserable.' She tilted her head back and clamped her lips around the water tube again.

Ben turned towards the door.

Kelly waved him back. 'No – don't go. I either talk to you or I watch endless news reports about the fire. Come and sit down. Where's your mum?'

Ben pulled up a chair and sat down next to the bed. 'She's busy. She's obsessed by finding out all she can about that US base we found.'

'Oh yeah? Why?'

'I told her about the big dome and she thought that sounded odd for a listening station. She made some calls. It turns out it's some kind of top secret research place. Just like the protestors said.'

Kelly bristled. She clearly felt that any criticism of Americans was a personal attack on her. 'Oh yeah? What are we meant to be researching?'

'Weather control.'

'Weather control? I've never heard anything so far-fetched!' She folded her arms defensively, then remembered she had a drip in her arm and looked down in alarm in case she had dislodged it. 'Stop thinking that because we're the most powerful nation on the planet we've got a god complex.'

Ben wasn't surprised that she found it all incredible. He'd had trouble believing it himself. 'Apparently it's not so far-fetched. It's called the High Active Auroral Research Project. They have technology that can make wind and rain and even tornadoes. Do you remember those scientists thought we'd come over in that big plane from Alaska? That's where the other HAARP research station is based. They've been shipping HAARP equipment to Australia.'

Kelly folded her arms tighter. 'Baloney. I thought your mother was a scientist, not another of these kooky activists. Give me a break.' She was starting to get angry.

'My mum got this from respected scientists, not crackpots.' Ben leaned forward. 'Listen, in Alaska, a lot of people living near the HAARP station have been getting weird illnesses . . . and their dogs and cats were dying. Does that sound familiar? That was happening in Coober Pedy.'

'According to a bunch of hairy, sandal-wearing, mud-wallowing bums. People get sick all the time. That doesn't prove anything.' Kelly ended up coughing again, a long attack that turned her face red.

'Look, I'm telling you because you might need to get checked out by a doctor. If you don't believe me, that's fine. This HAARP thing fires a super-charged, high-frequency radio wave into the sky. It's like detonating a nuclear bomb in the ionosphere. The fallout can give people migraines, allergies . . . I just thought you might want to know—' Ben stopped. Kelly was waving her hand at the mask.

'Oxygen.'

Ben stood up, pulled the mask down and put it over her nose. She took some deep, slow breaths, then nodded that she'd had enough. Ben took the mask away and sat down again.

Kelly leaned forward and pulled her knees up beneath the sheets, hugging them. She looked like she was thinking seriously about what he had said. 'When we were near the base,' she said in a small voice, 'it got very windy and I thought I was covered in crawling insects. And then you got it too.'

Ben nodded. 'And the plane instruments went haywire. I said it felt like an electric shock. HAARP can also knock out communications systems. Apparently that's another reason the military are interested in it. We definitely got hit by fallout from this thing.'

Kelly shuddered and hugged her knees tighter. 'Did you see a doctor? What did they say?'

'The doctor couldn't find anything wrong.'

Actually, that wasn't the whole truth. The doctor who examined Ben hadn't had experience of that type of radiation. Bel was trying to find some experts who did.

'I expect your mum's got everyone running around in a panic. At least the base is in the middle of Australia, so it can't be harming that many people.'

Ben shook his head. 'That's not what Mum says. She thinks they chose Australia for a more sinister reason. Alaska has given them control of weather in the northern hemisphere. Australia gives them the South Pole too. It's like a world domination thing. She's gone straight to the Australian prime minister about it.'

'It sounds like we stumbled on something pretty big,' said Kelly thoughtfully.

'Big and sinister. I thought we were chasing red herrings out there in the desert, but we might just have blown the lid on research that could be as dangerous as the hydrogen bomb.'

Kelly looked down at her knees, deep in thought. 'Remind me, what's your mom's organization called? Fragile Planet, isn't it?'

'Yes,' said Ben.

'I'm thinking maybe I should join. Can you ask her?'

Ben snorted. 'If I ever see her. On top of the half-term break, I only got a few extra days holiday off school so I've got to fly back home in a few days. She's working round the clock again. I might as well have stayed in Britain.'

Kelly smiled weakly. 'That's like my dad. I'd just caught up with him here in Melbourne, and he immediately had to go off somewhere on army business.'

'Does he know we – er – wrecked the microlight?'

Kelly sat bolt upright, her eyes wide. 'No way. And I'm not going to tell him we broke into a top secret base either.' She lay back against the pillow. 'Hey – at least you have some good stories to tell about your holiday. You're getting to be something of an expert on disaster zones, what with the flood in London and now this.'

Ben suddenly started laughing. He laughed so hard that tears ran down his cheeks. It was almost a minute before he could compose himself enough to talk again.

Kelly was looking at him, mystified. 'What did I say?'

Ben sighed. 'My whole family is one big disaster zone.'

Epilogue

Out in the Great Victoria Desert, Grishkevich and Hijkoop had quite a crowd in their lab. Most of the base's science personnel, and a visitor, had gathered around one of the TV monitors to watch a news broadcast.

The screen showed two firefighters moving slowly through a blackened building, searching the ground with powerful torches. They moved unsteadily, the wet wreckage sliding and shifting under their feet. Where it had moved, smoke rose in wisps from the deeper layers. The surface was cooling, but underneath it was still hot.

A journalist gave a commentary: '*The first fires in Adelaide were reported at eleven this morning. By two o'clock most of the city was on fire. It burned until eight this evening – and experts say if it hadn't been for a freak thunderstorm it might still be burning now. For many it has been a lucky escape, but the search for casualties goes on . . .*'

Hijkoop stabbed a button and the screen went blank. He turned round. 'How about that? Saved because the weather changed. That's the power of nature for you. And that is why we have to be able to control it.'

His remark was addressed mainly to their guest. He was a commanding presence – tall, and wearing charcoal-blue dress uniform with gold buttons.

Major Kurtis spoke: 'Gentlemen, I am totally in agreement. I am here to tell you that despite anything you may hear to the contrary, the HAARP experiment is very far from over.'

If you enjoyed this book, you'll also enjoy the *Alpha Force* series by Chris Ryan. Turn over to read the beginning of *Red Centre*, which is also set in Australia!

Extract from Alpha Force: Red Centre
Copyright © Chris Ryan, 2004
0 099 46424 1
978 0 099 46424 2

Fun and Games

Being up the tree wasn't the scary part. It was OK if you looked straight ahead at what was in front of your nose. All you saw was the trunk, which was solid, gnarled and rough, with warty areas like the hide of a prehistoric animal. In places Hex could see tiny cracks, where a softer, redder substance showed through the bark. It smelled warm and woody and wet. In fact everywhere was warm and wet. Hex's clothes were drenched with sweat and when he breathed in, the air was damp like steam.

The trouble started if you looked anywhere but straight ahead. Not down – Hex knew better than to look down – but on either side. Then he saw thin air and foliage fading into a blue haze in the far distance and his senses started turning somersaults.

He felt his teeth baring in a fierce grin that was outside his control. It was partly nervousness, partly a sense of the absurdity of his position. Here he was, suspended ten metres up a red cedar tree in the Australian rainforest with his foot on a branch, waiting for the signal to swing on a rope to the next tree. A week earlier Hex hadn't even realized Australia had thick jungles like this. Now he knew – thanks to an online virtual tour while waiting to board his plane – that the vast continent harboured a great variety of terrains, and many extremes. Here at the very tip of the Daintree Rainforest in Queensland all was lush, wet and tropical. Hex knew that only ten or so kilometres away, the land became arid and the trees shrivelled to scrub and bush.

Hex focused on the tree he was clinging to, then swivelled his head slowly like an owl, careful not to risk a disorientating glance up or down. His gaze found the next tree, his destination. A bright yellow star-shaped target glittering there, pinned between two branches.

Together with four friends from far-flung corners of the globe, Hex was part of the group they called Alpha Force. They had tackled many arduous missions together but this had to be one of the strangest – volunteering to try out a series of games for a reality TV show. It's for charity, Hex reminded himself soberly, forcing the grin off his face before it turned into hysteria. For every star collected, a sponsor would pay money to a chosen charity, and so Alpha Force were here doing a trial run before the real contestants arrived.

Hex wasn't entirely in his element. The kind of games he excelled at involved codes and were firmly grounded in cyberspace: he was an expert hacker and code-breaker. His natural habitat was indoors, at his computer or in the gym. When he wasn't on a mission with Alpha Force, the only contact he had with the great outdoors was running and cycling across Hampstead Heath. But here he was, hanging up a tree in a steamy rainforest, waiting for the camera crew to finalize their positions and lighting.

The other members of Alpha Force weren't having it any easier. As Hex was edging his feet nervously along the branch, his Anglo-Chinese friend Li was hurtling towards the ground twenty metres away at the end of a bungee rope. Unlike Hex, though, Li most definitely *was* in her element. She was grasping the rope with both hands with her knees bent and her feet out ready for the impact. The moment she touched down on the forest floor, she folded at the waist and knees and then sprang up like a cat, propelling herself towards a box high up in another tree. The move was graceful and smooth, and executed with the pinpoint accuracy of one who has trained as an athlete from an early age. The tight plait of Li's long black silky hair sailed out behind her like a tail and her slim legs caught a branch with the ease of a trapeze artist. She wrapped her legs around it and steadied herself while she reached into the box for one of the yellow stars. Then, like a monkey, she dropped back down to the ground and lifted off again in one slick movement.

Paulo would have been happy right then to have joined his friends in the trees. He was on his hands and knees in a Perspex tunnel which was like a greenhouse in the fierce Australian heat. Brushing sweat out of his eyes with his wrist, Paulo came across one of the yellow stars and grabbed it, eager to finish the game trial and get back out into fresh air – or, at any rate, fresher air; the whole rainforest was like a sauna at this time of day. On Paulo's list of priorities right at that moment, saving the tiger from extinction ran a distant second to gulping down an ice-cold cola float.

Paulo lifted the target. 'Got it!' he called to the camera crew.

The first thing that hit him was an angry droning noise. On the earth in front of him, a black shape was spreading like treacle. Was it tar? Oil? Paulo had a split-second when he noted with curiosity that the black stuff glinted with a blue metallic sheen, and then a cloud of huge flies hurtled up into his face like missiles. They buzzed around his ears and pelted his skin, seeking out the sweat that dripped off him in a constant flow. He let out a splutter and they swarmed into his open mouth. He felt a crunching sensation, a bitter taste, and spat violently, shaking his head and then his whole body in an effort to dislodge them.

Crunched flies stuck between his lips and teeth. The walls of the tunnel rocked from side to side. It made no difference. The flies were glued to the sweat on his face like a black lace veil. They began to swarm down under his collar and creep up his sleeves.

Paulo had reckoned he was fairly used to flies: on his ranch in Argentina flies and other insects were a constant torment to the livestock and the people who handled them. But this was something else.

'Who dreams up TV shows like this anyway?' he muttered under his breath as he crawled doggedly on into the next chamber. This was hung with spider webs. Maybe webs were just what he needed to deal with the flies, Paulo thought.

The webs stuck to him like sticky muslin, but he barely noticed against all the droning and fizzing in his ears. He lifted the next target and under it was a large spider.

Paulo grimaced at the spider. 'I'll swap you that star for all these delicious flies – how about that?' he said.

'Hold it there, Paulo,' called one of the camera technicians. 'We need to set up the close-up on the spider. Won't take a second.'

Paulo waited, grumbling to himself in his native Spanish. He wasn't too squeamish about wildlife, but this spider wasn't exactly his first choice of company in a confined space. Its body was dark and torpedo-shaped and marked with fine yellow flecks. Its legs were as long as Paulo's fingers and sported yellow bands. They shifted and fidgeted and Paulo imagined hypodermic needles ready to offload poison. Not that it would really be poisonous, of course. Not in a TV game show; Paulo knew that. He just had to keep telling himself.

'Sorry, Paulo,' called the technician. 'This is going to take longer than we thought. Make yourself comfortable.'

'Looks like we're stuck with each other,' Paulo told the spider wryly. 'Got any yarns you'd like to spin while we wait?'

Alex meanwhile was also crawling – even more uncomfortably. He was on his hands and knees in a trench that had been turned into a miniature swamp, complete with weeds and leeches – and an authentically rank smell. As Alex moved along he felt the bottom for the tell-tale hard edges of a yellow star. Actually, although the trench was most people's idea of hell, Alex didn't find it too unpleasant. It reminded him of stories his father had told him. Alex's dad was in the SAS, and survival lore – along with deliciously hair-raising stories of SAS selection – had been as natural a part of Alex's upbringing and education as football and double maths.

Alex's fingers found a target under the mud and he yanked it up, pulling it free of the weeds. The mud slurped thickly and released a pungent gust of gas – a clammy, rotting smell that caught the back of Alex's throat and made him gag. He paused and closed his eyes tightly, willing the nausea to pass. His dad had once told him how he had had to crawl through a sewer on a covert mission in Colombia – or maybe it was after a night on the tiles in Glasgow? Either way, Alex told himself he would have to be prepared for anything if he was to follow in his father's footsteps.

The mud was up to his shoulders and hips at this point and felt like thick warm slurry inside his T-shirt and shorts, but Alex looked on the bright side: at least it kept the mosquitoes away. He paused and slicked some of the mud over his face and neck like camouflage cream. This would be heaven if I was a hippo, he thought.

A short time later, the fifth member of the team, Amber, was wading chest-deep in a lake a few hundred metres away, making her way towards a clump of reeds where she could see a star target. Fronds of water weed brushed against her bare legs and occasionally she felt something more solid slither past, but that might have been her imagination. She was wearing her walking boots, so she felt fairly well protected. On the whole she was finding the games good fun. The lake formed an open clearing in the heart of the jungle, and Amber was enjoying being out in the sun, her black skin soaking up the rays greedily. It was the first time she'd seen the sun since Alpha Force had arrived in the rainforest the day before. So far they'd stayed under the immense canopy of trees; even at high noon it was like a dark, damp underworld. The green light filtering in shifting patterns through the leaves had reminded her of scuba-diving in the gloom of the ocean floor. Now she felt as if she had swum up and broken through the surface.

Water was a natural habitat for Amber. She was as much at home *on* water as *in* it. Her parents had been software billionaires and had owned several yachts. As well as being an expert sailor, she was proficient at all water sports, skiing, horse riding and archery,. After her parents had died in a plane crash, Amber had discovered that they were a good deal more adventurous than she had ever imagined. Secretly they had put their skills and wealth to good use, exposing human rights abuses and smuggling film from oppressive regimes to newsrooms around the world. Amber had led a sheltered rich-kid existence up till then. Now she, like Alex, was determined to uphold the family tradition.

As Amber untangled the first target, she caught sight of Hex at the water's edge. He must have finished his game. Let's see how alert he is, she thought. With a flick of the wrist she frisbeed the target out of the lake.

Hex caught it in a smooth movement. 'You throw like a girl,' he shouted.

'Yeah? You catch like a geek,' said Amber, flashing him a grin.

Tracey, a production executive in her early twenties, was standing on the bank waving her wide-brimmed bush hat. 'Over there, Amber.'

Amber looked round. There was a second yellow star on a rock a little way off. She set off towards it, wading purposefully.

On the bank, Hex tapped Tracey on the shoulder. 'Excuse me, but have you seen that?' He pointed to a clump of reeds. A crocodile skulked low in the water, its rough back glistening in the sun like a wet log. Its half-closed eye was just visible above the water line.

Tracey looked up from her clipboard and peered at Hex over the top of her rimless glasses. 'It's not a real crocodile,' she said in a laboriously patient tone, as if talking to a small child rather than a teenager with genius-level IQ. She pointed to other dark shapes in the water. 'Look – there, and there. They're just props. Plastic.'

'I can see those other ones are plastic,' replied Hex. 'But I just came up from that direction and there wasn't a crocodile there then.'

Tracey gave him a condescending smile. 'They're plastic,' she said again. 'That means they float, and they tend to drift around a bit once people wade in and start stirring up the water.'

Another target came whizzing across. Hex caught it on reflex, even though he hadn't been looking. As he turned, he noticed a couple of men in green ranger uniforms standing near the water's edge holding what looked like tranquillizer guns.

'Smart catch,' said Tracey.

'Are they for authenticity too?' said Hex, nodding towards the men.

'Yes, we're going to use them during filming. It makes the audience think it's all for real, you see.'

Amber was wading towards a third star target when she stopped abruptly.

Hex instantly tensed. Something caused the hairs on his neck to prickle. 'Amber, you OK?' he called.

'My foot's stuck in some weed,' replied Amber. Hex could see her shoulders jerk as she pulled hard. But she didn't move. 'Darn,' she muttered. 'Must be caught on my boot.' She jerked her foot again, harder.

Hex's uneasy feeling hadn't gone away. He looked

over to the crocodile again. It looked much the same as it had before. Or did it? Hex had an excellent eye for detail. He could explore high security computer systems and erase all trace that he had been there. He had learned to trust his instincts. *Think*, he told himself. *What's wrong with this picture?*

He looked at the other crocs. They were just as low in the water as the one he'd noticed, moving from side to side in the ripples created as Amber tried to pull her foot free.

And then Hex realized what was wrong. All the other crocodiles were moving. But this one was dead still. It was real! It had sensed that Amber was in trouble and was stalking her.

In the water, Amber swore again, took a deep breath and sank below the surface.

Hex yelled at the top of his lungs, 'Amber, no!'

In the murky depths, Amber didn't hear him. She couldn't see a thing either. She had kicked up so much silt that the water was like vegetable soup. She groped around her ankle and felt the rope-like weed that had snared her foot. Her fingers explored it and she found a thick section, with some thinner fronds that had caught on the hooks of her boots. She was stuck fast.

Breathing out hard, Amber surfaced. The first thing she heard was Hex shouting furiously: 'Amber! Get out of the water! There's a crocodile!'

Amber's head shot round. She saw Hex waving his arms frantically, while Tracey was rooted to the spot. Next to them, the rangers were raising tranquillizer guns to their shoulders. Her heart pounding, Amber followed the line of the barrels and saw a dark shape, low in the water. She yanked her foot hard but it remained tethered to the bottom. She was helpless – an animal in a trap.

Tracey was crying, her voice hysterical. 'It's no good. The guns aren't loaded yet!'

'It's my boot,' shrieked Amber. 'I'm going to try to get it off.'

Hex saw Amber sink down again. Keeping her head above the water, she was feeling for her bootlaces. Her face was a mask of desperation as she scrabbled to undo them. Hex knew the type of boots Amber wore. They were built for strenuous outdoor hiking, durable as Kevlar and tightly fixed around her ankles with criss-crossed lacing. When the others were waiting for

Amber to get ready, they often complained about how fiddly those boots were. 'That's the whole point,' she always said. 'I know they aren't going to come off in a hurry.'

Now those reliable boots had become a death trap.

'The croc's gone,' said one of the rangers. He lowered his gun warily.

'It's underwater somewhere,' said the other ranger.

Amber's fingers must have worked like lightning. She was free of her boot and powering towards them in a strong front crawl.

'Go, Amber, go!' shrilled Tracey. She was jumping up and down in almost a cartoon parody of panic.

With a hungry crocodile in the water behind her, Amber needed no encouragement. She hit the lake edge, and all eyes were on her as she splashed through the reeds and out onto the shore. Weals showed bright red on her dark skin where her leg had been cut into by the cable-hard weeds. She scrabbled across the mud and collapsed at Hex's feet, gasping.

'Where is it . . . ?'

Tracey stepped closer to the water's edge and peered down. 'It's gone,' she said. She turned and looked back at them with a smile. 'Vanished. We must have scared it off.'

Realization hit Hex like a thunderbolt. He moved back, dragging Amber with him. 'Get away from the edge!' he shrieked. 'Get away!'

Tracey turned, puzzled. At that moment the water beside her exploded as the crocodile erupted from the lake like a missile. Hex saw the great hinged jaws out-lined in a spray of water. It was a sight to inspire shock and awe: a gaping prehistoric mouth filled with uneven reptile fangs. It was a frozen fragment of time, an uncanny glimpse into a Jurassic morning.

Adrenaline made Hex move like Max Payne in bullet time. He seized one of the useless tranquilliser guns. Swinging it directly over his head like a kendo stick, he brought it down with all his strength. The blow landed solidly on the soft part of the crocodile's nose. The reptile twisted round, still with a fixed expression of cold-blooded glee, and hit the water with a heavy splash.

'Run!' yelled Hex. This time nobody bothered to ask questions. As one, the party raced for the tree line. Hex knew that the croc might possibly follow them onto the lake shore, but one glance back told him that it had had enough. It was heading back towards the centre of the lake.

Then they stood, leaning on trees, panting and gasping, as they got their breath back. Tracey was on all fours, her stomach heaving in and out like bellows, her eyes wide and horrified.

Amber fell to her knees and then rolled onto her backside. 'Ow, my foot,' she yelped, sitting up and inspecting her bare sole. 'I've trodden on something I shouldn't have.'

One of the rangers looked at her. 'I thought you'd had it there, girl.'

Hex stretched out flat on the ground and let out a long sigh. 'It wasn't Amber it wanted after all. It was more interested in the people standing on the shore.'

'I feel quite offended,' said Amber, laughing in sheer relief. 'What is it? Don't I look tasty? Not enough fat on me, or what?'

'Oh my God,' said Tracey to Hex. 'You just saved our lives.'

'Yeah . . . ' Amber looked at him, shaking her head slowly. 'How did you know to do that?'

'I thought I'd better learn a martial art so I took advantage of a cut-price, fourteen-day holiday at the Shaolin Temple,' said Hex.

Amber gave him her sternest look.

Hex propped himself up on his elbow and grinned. 'OK, I saw it in a game.'

They were all quiet for a moment. Then Amber said brightly, 'Well, the next game is to find my lost boot. Any volunteers?'

About the Author

CHRIS RYAN joined the SAS in 1984 and has been involved in numerous operations with the Regiment. During the first Gulf War he was the only member of an eight-man team to escape from Iraq, three colleagues being killed and four captured. It was the longest escape and evasion in the history of the SAS. For this he was awarded the Military Medal. He wrote about his remarkable escape in *The One Who Got Away* (1995), which was also adapted for screen.

He left the SAS in 1994 and is now the author of many bestselling thrillers for adults, as well as the *Alpha Force* series for younger readers. His work in security takes him around the world and he has also appeared in a number of television series, including *Hunting Chris Ryan*, in which his escape and evasion skills were demonstrated to the max, and *Pushed to the Limit*, in which Chris put ordinary British families through a series of challenges. More recently, he appeared in *Terror Alert* on Sky TV, demonstrating his skills in a range of different scenarios.

Wildfire is the second title in a new series of thrillers for younger readers: *Code Red* adventures.

ALPHA FORCE – THE MISSIONS
Have you read them all . . . ?

SURVIVAL The five members of Alpha Force meet for the first time when they survive a shipwreck and are marooned on a desert island.

RAT-CATCHER Alpha Force fight to catch an evil drugs baron in South America.

DESERT PURSUIT Alpha Force come face-to-face with a gang of child-slavers operating in the Sahara Desert.

HOSTAGE When they are alerted to reports of illegal dumping of toxic waste, Alpha Force fly to Canada to investigate.

RED CENTRE An Australian bushfire and a hunted terrorist test Alpha Force's skills to the limit.

HUNTED Alpha Force find themselves in a desperate battle with a ruthless band of ivory poachers in Zambia.

BLOOD MONEY While they are in southern India, Alpha Force learn of a growing trade in organ transplants from living donors and must locate a young girl before it's too late.

FAULT LINE Disaster strikes when a massive earthquake devastates a built-up area in Belize.

BLACK GOLD Alpha Force are diving in the Caribbean when an oil tanker runs aground and an assassin strikes.

UNTOUCHABLE Alpha Force must unearth the truth about the mysterious activity on a laird's estate in the Scottish Highlands.